D0167007

DATE DUE

GAYLORD   PRINTED IN U.S.A.

STORM RUNNERS

BARBARA MITCHELHILL

Andersen Press
London

First published in 2007 by
Andersen Press Limited,
20 Vauxhall Bridge Road, London SW1V 2SA
www.andersenpress.co.uk

Reprinted 2008

British Library Cataloguing in Publication Data available

ISBN 978 184 270 640 4

Typeset by FiSH Books, Enfield, Middx.
Printed and bound in Great Britain by Bookmarque Ltd.,
Croydon, Surrey

For my splendiferous granddaughters Louise and Lucy,
their devoted dog, Eddie, and their unflappable pony,
Bonnie, who have never trekked across Scotland and
have never come face to face with killer vultures but
who bravely camped out together in the garden
last summer.

Acknowledgements

With thanks to Liz Maude, my amazing editor, whose suggestions were invaluable and whose knowledge of boats proved critical. To Isabel and Fran Bennett, Ian Bradley, Louise Chambers, Anna Ellis-Rees and Sam Ponnaih, who read the early drafts of the book with such enthusiasm and gave feedback which was seriously helpful. Also to Sean Bradley and Janet Dicks, who were great sources of information about Edinburgh.

Chapter One

We were in Grandad's cellar when the storm started – just me, my sister Kirstie and our dog Lizzie. All we heard was the distant rumble of thunder, at first – and that didn't bother us. Why would it? But we started to get nervous when the lights began to flicker like in those old movies. They gave a sort of flash. Flicker... flash... flicker... flash... over and over.

And then they went out.

We couldn't see a thing. It was as black as treacle down there.

'*This is so annoying!*' said Kirstie. 'I've probably lost all the work I've done today on the laptop. How will I ever finish my novel if things like this keep happening? It's so not fair!'

'Calm down, sis. It's a power cut, not the end of the world. It'll come back on in a few minutes.'

'Maybe.'

'We could go up to the kitchen, if you like.'

'No, I'm not moving, Alexandra. I'm staying put.'

The truth was that Kirstie, who pretended to be sooooo grown up, knew that if she crossed the cellar she might walk into some of those droopy cobwebs that hung from the ceiling, they might cling to her face and spiders might drop on her. She'd squeal like ten pigs – I just knew it. Creepy-crawlies were not her thing.

'Right then,' I said. 'We'll wait here.'

We didn't speak for a while. I was thinking about my amazing new ammonite when Kirstie suddenly yelled, 'Oh my God! What if the storm brought down the power line to the cottage? What will we do, Ally?'

My sister always thinks the worst. 'Don't panic,' I said. 'We'll manage.'

'If Dad was here, he'd know what to do, wouldn't he? He'd get the lights fixed.'

'Well, he isn't here,' I said. 'He'll be on the mainland by now. Don't throw a wobbly, Kirstie. The storm will blow over and the lights will come back on any minute. OK?'

I heard her give one of her dramatic sighs and we waited for several minutes. I tried to look at my watch but I couldn't even see my hand in front of my face.

Eventually, Kirstie burst out, 'It's no good. I've changed my mind. I can't stand the dark any longer. Let's get out of here and go over to the Camerons'. They won't mind.'

The Camerons lived in the farm over the hill. Dad had arranged that we could go there for tea while he went to see our grandad. Last week (just before we left Edinburgh to spend our holiday with him) Grandad had telephoned from a call box. He had sounded really spooked.

'I've lived on Shairn all ma life,' he'd said, 'but I cannae stay a minute longer. There are things going on.'

He wouldn't say what was going on exactly, but he had left the island and gone to live in an old stone hut on the mainland. Weird or what? We'd asked him to go back but he'd said no. Dad was really worried. He thought Grandad was going crazy or something.

We still packed our things and set off for Grandad's cottage – even though he had gone AWOL.

'We'll go and see him and persuade him to come back,' Dad said, the day we arrived on the island. 'He needs looking after. We'll catch the first ferry in the morning, eh?'

'*We* don't have to go, do we, Dad?' I'd said. 'Grandad won't listen to us. He's gone completely batty. Can't we stay and play in the cellar? No messing.

3

Honest! Please, please, please let us. I desperately need to finish cataloguing my fossil collection.'

'Oh yes,' Kirstie had said. 'Dad, please let us. You promised I could use your laptop. I'm at a really, really important chapter in my novel. Pleeeeeeeeeeeeeease.'

In the end, Dad let us stay. Kirstie was fourteen after all. But part of the deal was that we would go over to the Camerons' at four o' clock.

So we had decided not to hang around in the cellar waiting for the power to come on. We would go to the farm.

'OK,' I said. 'But I want to take my catalogue to show the Camerons. They both like fossils. Hang on till I get it.'

In the dark, I felt along the shelf for the book, when a thunderclap sounded overhead and Lizzie began to whine.

'The storm seems to be getting worse, Ally,' said Kirstie. 'We'll get soaked going over the fields and my hair will be ruined.'

'Never mind your hair, I thought . . .'

More thunder interrupted me. It was so loud that Kirstie screamed and Lizzie pushed past my legs and curled up at my feet, shivering.

Quickly, I tried to find my catalogue but, before I could, thunder cracked overhead again. This time it was loud enough to shatter eardrums, break glass, make anybody freak out. I flung myself to the ground and grabbed Lizzie. Kirstie screamed again – and I did, just a bit.

But it was only the start. After that, the thunder came crashing, rolling, rumbling, booming.

There were a few seconds of quiet . . . no sound . . . no rumble . . . nothing. And we held our breath.

Then BAAANNNGGG!

Even with my fingers stuffed in my ears, even with my sweatshirt pulled over my head, I could hear it. The noise went on and on. It was crazy. The walls of the cellar were shaking. Mortar was falling from between the stones and filling the air with dust. We could feel it on our skin and – worse – we were breathing it in. Our lungs were getting clogged with it. Cough, cough, cough. We couldn't stop. Cough, cough, cough.

Then I felt Kirstie nearby, grabbing my arm. 'The walls could cave in. We've got to get out of here, Ally. NOW.' And she pulled me towards the steps.

Cough, cough, cough. We were so wracked with coughing that we could only climb slowly, step by step. Cough, cough, cough. Cough, cough, cough.

By the time we reached the top, the thunder had stopped. Had the storm blown over? I hoped so.

The dust was settling and soon we were able to breathe easily again. As I stood on the top step, I reached for the handle to open the door into the kitchen. But the door wouldn't budge. I tried again. This time I pushed it with my shoulder. The result was the same.

'What's the matter?' Kirstie asked. 'Hurry up, Ally. Let's get out of here.'

'The door won't open. It's stuck.'

Together we tried to force it. We pushed, we pulled, we hammered the door with our fists. But it would not open – not even the smallest crack.

As I stood there, feeling helpless, the truth suddenly dawned on me. Of course! If the storm was bad enough to shake the walls of the cellar, then the whole cottage had probably collapsed above us and behind the door there must be a mountain of rubble.

If I was right, how were we going to get out of the cellar?

Chapter Two

We had tried everything to open the door. There seemed to be nothing we could do.

'There's no point in messing about any more, Ally,' said Kirstie. 'I'll ring for help. My mobile's on the bench.'

In the dark, she went slowly down the steps with Lizzie, who was keen to help, as always. But my sister wasn't in the best of moods.

'Get out of my way, girl. I'll trip over you. Ally! Keep hold of the dog, will you?'

I called Lizzie while Kirstie felt her way around the walls of the cellar.

'Watch out what you're doing, Kirst.' My sister could be very clumsy and I was worried about my collection. 'Don't mess up. I've spent ages getting those fossils in order.' I listened out for any accidents but there were no crashes or anything. Just as well!

'I can't find my mobile...but it should be somewhere...on the desk.' I could hear her patting the bench, trying to find it. 'Here's the laptop,' she said. 'I know I put the phone next to it...Ah, got it. Great. GERONIMO!'

What happened next was Kirstie's fault. She shouldn't have got so excited and yelled like that. When she freaked out, so did Lizzie, and she went dashing down the steps. I couldn't stop her, could I?

CRASH!

'OW! Lizzie! No! YOU CRAZY DOG!'

'What's happened?'

'She knocked the phone onto the floor. Would you believe it?'

Of course I couldn't see a thing.

'What are you doing?'

'I'm on my hands and knees, trying to find it.'

'Shall I come and help?'

'No. Stay there. You might stand on it. If I'm careful, I'll get it. It can't be far away.'

I could hear her patting her hand on the stone floor, feeling for the phone.

'Have you got it?'

'No...but if I stretch out further...I might get it...'

Finally she yelled, 'I've got it, Ally. Phew, thank goodness. Right. Now I'll ring the Camerons. Get them to come across.'

I heard her flick open her mobile and I waited.

'It's not working.'

'Is it switched on?'

'Of course it is. I always switch it on as soon as I get up.' She paused but nothing happened. 'Oh well, perhaps I didn't this morning.'

She couldn't see in the dark, of course, but she pressed what she thought was the ON button and waited – but the screen did not light up as it usually did. It didn't play the little tune and say 'hello' either. She tried a different button, then the one next to that – all with the same result. Not a bleep. Not a light. Nothing.

'It's no good. It's dead!'

'I bet you forgot to charge it. That's dumb, Kirstie. We're in a right mess now – all because you forgot.'

'Excuse me! *I did not forget*. I put it on charge every night.'

'Then you must have smashed it when you dropped it.'

'I didn't drop it. Lizzie knocked it out of my hand. So don't blame me.'

The argument went on for ages but it didn't make any difference, did it? We still couldn't ring out.

'What other bright ideas have you got, O Mighty Teenage Brainbox?'

9

Kirstie stayed over by the laptop – she was in a right mood. I stayed on the steps, furious that my sister couldn't do the simplest thing like charging her phone. Lizzie trotted backwards and forwards between the two of us wanting to be let out. We'd been down there for hours.

'Well actually,' Kirstie said, 'I don't think we need to do anything. We just stay here.'

'Oh yes? Do we just make a wish and let the good fairy whisk us away?'

'Don't be so annoying.'

'I'm not the one who's annoying.'

'Think about it, Ally. When we don't arrive at four o' clock, Mr and Mrs Cameron will come over to fetch us. Or they might phone and when there's no answer, they'll think something's wrong. Whichever way, they'll come.'

'Maybe.'

'Just remember, they're officially keeping an eye on us until Dad gets back.'

Having said all we wanted to say, we sat in silence and it was then that we heard the trickle of water in the far corner and the stench of dog pee filled the cellar.

Chapter Three

That was all I needed. Sitting in the dark in a cellar with the stink of dog pee.

'Gross,' said Kirstie. 'I'm going to be sick.'

'She can't help it. Anyway, has it crossed your mind that we might need to go to the toilet before long – and there isn't one?'

She gave one of her long sighs.

'...and another thing...' I said.

'What?' she snapped.

'We might run out of air.'

'Don't, Ally! That's seriously scary.'

'Well, I'm not sitting here waiting for somebody to come and rescue us,' I said, getting to my feet. 'I'm going to break that door down.'

'How? We've tried everything.'

'Grandad's tools are hanging on the wall by his workbench. There must be something we can use.'

Through the darkness, I felt my way across to where I thought the workbench was.

'I'll get a hammer,' I said.

'Don't bother. I know where the tools are,' Kirstie called out as she headed the same way.

'Leave it. I'll be there before you.'

I didn't want Kirstie to get there first, so I wasn't as careful as I should have been, I suppose. I was side-stepping along the wall when my right foot suddenly shot from under me and I yelled, 'Aaaaah!' I tried to stay upright. My arms flailed in the air like an old windmill. But in seconds my other foot skidded out of control and I crashed to the ground, flat on my back.

'Ally. Are you all right?'

'I think so,' I said as I lay there, checking my limbs for broken bones. It was then that I noticed something was seeping through my sweatshirt – spreading across my back – and I realised I had landed in Lizzie's puddle. I was soaking in the stuff.

I sat up and wrenched my sweatshirt over my head and frantically rubbed my back with the sleeves. Then I flung the disgusting garment away over into the corner.

'What are you doing?' Kirstie called across the cellar.

'Nothing,' I said. There was no way she was going to have a laugh at my expense.

'Right,' she said. 'Let's get something to open that door.'

I finally found a heavy lump hammer, went back up the stairs and managed to smash away the lock with two or three blows. Then I bent down to look through the hole it had left. It was just as we'd thought.

'There a humungous pile of rubble,' I said. 'There's no way we could open the door.'

'What now?'

'I'll try to smash a hole in it so we can climb out.'

I raised the hammer to strike at the wood, but before I could, Kirstie grabbed hold of it and pushed past me without even a please or a thank you.

'Leave it to me,' she said. 'I'm stronger than you.' She can be so bossy at times.

I went back down the steps, staying well clear of her while she swung the hammer again and again. BANG! SMASH! CRASH!

'It's giving way,' she yelled. 'One more go and it should split.'

When the final strike came, I heard the sound of tearing wood. Pieces broke away, so that light filtered through the hole and into the cellar and we could see again.

Beyond the door was a huge pile of stones and slate blocking our way out. Kirstie leaned forward and put her hand on the rubble. 'I'll try to push it away,' she called down to me. But pushing the stones was the worst thing she could have done because as soon as she touched them, they began to move. I was well clear, but Kirstie was in the path of the rubble as it burst through the hole like an avalanche, cascading down the steps, engulfing her in a waterfall of stones.

Chapter Four

I grabbed Lizzie and flung myself against the wall as the bricks and stones fell. Clouds of dust rose and I squeezed my eyes shut until it had settled. When I opened them again, I saw that the cellar steps were covered in rubble but – worse – a great heap of it was lying at the bottom, and my sister was under it.

'Kirstie!' I yelled as I scrambled across the debris. 'Kirstie! Kirstie!' I began tearing at the bricks, flinging them behind me. The pile was almost a metre high. She wouldn't be able to breathe under it. The weight alone could crush her ribs. If I had any chance of saving her, I would have to work fast. I grabbed and pushed and heaved and pulled. I clawed the biggest pieces out of the way – on and on, stone after stone, until my fingers were bleeding. But at last I uncovered her face. It was plastered with thick grey powder, eyes closed and stock still. I bent close and listened and found that she was breathing. Thank goodness. She wasn't dead – but she was unconscious.

Resuming my frantic pace, I cleared more stones until Kirstie's body was free of the weight. I spoke her name as I wiped her face with my hand, cleaning it as best I could, and eventually she began to groan; then she coughed and opened her eyes. She tried to speak but the dust clogged her throat. All she could do was cough.

'You need water. I'll go up to the kitchen and get you some. Don't move.'

It was a stupid thing to say. She couldn't have moved if she had wanted to. She must have felt as if she had been in a fight with a steamroller.

'I won't be long.'

I began to climb with difficulty over the rubble. I had to find a firm foothold before I dared to lift a foot and move forward up the steps. My worst fear was that the stones would shift again and would fall on Kirstie.

I called down to her. 'Nearly there. I can almost touch the door. I'll be through any minute.'

The stones held firm, I stepped forward and grabbed hold of the broken wood of the cellar door and hung on. I was filled with relief and I leaned through the hole to take in a lungful of the air that was blowing through the cottage.

'I'm here, Kirstie. I've done it. We're going to be all right.'

I struggled through the hole and into the kitchen. Straight away I could see what the storm had done. It looked as if a giant fist had burst through the roof smashing everything below. One of the outside walls had been blasted away and the roof was gone. Only the chimney stood above it all, pointing to the sky in defiance. There were piles of stone and roof tiles, floorboards and broken furniture. I could hardly believe the devastation. The home where Grandad had lived for so many years was gone. It looked like a war zone.

One piece of luck though – the sink was still intact, although there were some broken plates left on the draining board. I clambered through the wreckage to reach it and turn on the tap. The water gushed from the pipe as if everything was normal. I cupped my hands and took a mouthful before going back to the cellar door

'Good news,' I shouted. 'The tap's working. You'll have a drink any minute now.'

I found an empty plastic bottle, filled it and wrapped it in a towel I'd found trapped under the wreck of the table.

'Here it comes,' I called and tossed it through the hole towards her. If it hit her, the towel would soften the blow. But my aim was pretty good, though I say it myself. The bottle fell near her shoulder, sending up a cloud of dust as it landed. Slowly, she reached out and took it. She drank a little, coughed a good deal and then struggled to get herself into a sitting position. 'Thanks,' she croaked and drank again, then poured some over her face and wiped it with the towel.

I went back to the tap and washed the cuts on my hands and arms. I found a sweater in the remains of my chest of drawers and pulled it on. Then I started moving the rubble heaped near to the cellar door. It was exhausting work but, when I'd cleared it and opened the cellar door, I felt great!

'Do you think you could move away from the bottom of the steps, Kirstie?' I called down to her. 'I need to clear this rubbish off the steps and I'll have to push most of it down. And keep hold of Lizzie, will you?'

She managed to shuffle a little way – moaning all the time.

'My foot feels really bad, Ally.'

'Just let me get rid of this stuff on the stairs and I'll be able to come down and take a look. I don't suppose it's serious.' I said that in case she was thinking that her leg had dropped off. She always imagined things were much worse than they really were.

I found the seat of a broken kitchen chair and used it to push pieces of brick and stone off the top step, which set the rest of the debris rolling, rumbling and bumping to join the pile already in the cellar. Some bits were left scattered on the steps but I worked my way down, picking them up and tossing away as I went. When I had reached the bottom step, I cleared a path through the heap so I could get to Kirstie.

My biggest problem was trying to keep Lizzie away. She was so glad I was back.

'Sit, girl. Let me look at Kirstie's foot, eh?' My instructions didn't register on Lizzie who jumped up and down and covered me with licks. I made a note to take her to dog training lessons when we got back to Edinburgh after the holiday.

'Let's have a look,' I said as I knelt down by Kirstie's side. But she screwed up her face when I tried to move her foot.

'DON'T!' she yelled. 'That's excruciating. Get my trainer off, Ally. It feels like a vice.'

I undid the laces and pulled the opening as wide

as I could and tugged to remove the shoe but Kirstie screamed with pain.

'That's unbearable,' she said through gritted teeth.

'I'll stop if you want.'

'No. Go on, Ally. It's got to come off.'

I pulled again and managed to get the trainer over her heel so that it fell to the floor. Kirstie rolled over, howling in agony. And when the pain eased off, she looked down at her fast-swelling foot.

'Try to wiggle your toes,' I said.

She tried but she couldn't.

'No. I can't. I can't. And the pain is awful.'

I thought she could have broken some bones in her foot or maybe her ankle.

'You need to go to the hospital.'

'I can't move.'

'We'll call the ambulance. Or the fire brigade. They're used to emergencies.'

'We've no phone.'

'But Mrs Cameron has. I'll go over to the farm and get help. She'll sort it out, Kirstie.'

Leaving her behind with Lizzie for company, I climbed the cellar steps and threaded my way through the ruins of the kitchen and out into the fresh air.

I was about to run up the hill in the direction of the Camerons' farm, when I heard a car coming up the hill. Could it be Dad? He wasn't due back till bedtime. Car doors slammed and I heard a man's voice on the far side of the cottage.

Not Dad. Definitely not Dad.

I listened but I couldn't make out what he said. Then someone else spoke – another man. His voice was very deep and growly like a bear and it made me nervous. So instead of calling out 'Hello,' or 'Will you help us?' I ducked down behind a low stone wall and hid. It was a gut reaction . . . a sixth sense . . . whatever you call it. But thank goodness I did.

I heard them clambering over the rubble and something else, too. The heavy panting of a dog straining at its lead. A minute later, the men were nearer and I was able to hear every word they said.

'Another success,' said the man with the scary voice. 'I'm impressed by this one.'

'A good result, Dr Frankwall, sir.'

I found a small gap in the wall and looked through. I saw two men standing close together, talking. One was holding a large dog on a chain lead. I'd never seen one like it. It looked vicious and wild – more like a wolf or a hyena than a dog.

The men were wearing black combat trousers and jackets with silver stitching on the shoulder which looked like a lightning flash – something like that. Although they were dressed in military gear, they didn't look like military men. There was something dangerous and secretive about them.

The one with the dog was much too fat to be a soldier. His huge stomach overhung his belt and he reminded me of a sumo wrestler, except sumo wrestlers don't carry guns and hold snarling dogs.

The other man – the one with the deep voice – was much taller, with black hair. He stood erect with his arms folded across his chest as if used to giving orders and being obeyed. From the way he spoke, I guessed he was in charge. He must be Dr Frankwall – but he looked more like Dracula to me.

'How many were living here?' he asked as he looked at the great heap of stone in front of him.

'Just an old man, sir.'

'Mmmm. I doubt he's survived this.'

'Shall I send the dog in?'

He paused for a moment. 'Don't think we need to,' he said. 'Everything seems in order. Good.'

GOOD? Did he really say 'good'? What was good

about finding a cottage in ruins? For all he knew, Grandad could be under it. Didn't he care?

None of this made sense. But of one thing I was certain, I needed to keep well hidden. My heart was pounding against my ribs. BOOM. BOOM. BOOM. It was so loud I was scared stiff they'd hear it.

'There's the farm to check, sir,' said the Sumo Wrestler. 'It's about two miles from here but still in the target zone.' And he pointed in the direction of the Camerons' farm.

Then the worst possible thing happened. The dog spotted me behind the wall – or smelled me, more like. He lunged forward in my direction, barking fiercely and baring his teeth.

'Stop, Nero,' yelled Sumo and yanked the dog so hard on its chain that its front legs lifted off the ground. Then he kicked its rump with his great black boot and the dog yelped.

'He's after rabbits,' Sumo smirked. 'Wants his dinner. I keep him hungry. He's more use to me that way.'

Dracula looked irritated. 'Just keep him under control, that's all. Now let's go.'

As they were turning to leave, Dracula's mobile rang. He flicked it open, lifted it to his ear and listened.

'Stay where you are, sergeant,' he said into the phone. 'I want to see for myself.'

He clicked it shut. 'We'll forget the farm for now. I need to meet up with B Squad. Slight problem. We might have to move to the mainland sooner than we thought.' They started to walk away. 'The next test,' Dracula said, 'could be our last.'

What test? Who were these men and why were they here? And what were they going to do on the mainland? A hundred questions whizzed around my head – and I somehow knew that if I did find the answers, I would be very, very scared.

Chapter Five

When I heard the engine start up again and I was sure they had gone, I ran back into the ruin of Grandad's cottage. I scrambled over the debris and down the cellar steps.

'Kirstie!' I yelled. 'Kirstie! You'll never guess what I've seen.'

I hurried over to where she was lying in the corner.

'What?' She looked miserable and not all that interested. But I suppose she was concentrating on her foot. It was gross. All swollen like a pink football.

'Wait till I tell you,' I said. 'You won't believe it. I've just seen two men.'

Now she was interested. She tried to sit up. She even tried to smile. 'So someone's coming to help us. Thank goodness. That's brilliant news, Ally.'

I shook my head. 'No it isn't. They're horrible.'

She wrinkled her nose. 'What do you mean "horrible"?'

'They're really scary. They were dressed in black uniforms.'

'So they're soldiers, Ally. Grow up. What's the problem? What did they say? Where are they?'

'They didn't say anything to me! They didn't know I was there. I was hiding behind the wall.'

Kirstie went absolutely bananas.

'We're trapped down here,' she yelled, 'waiting for someone to get us out and YOU HIDE BEHIND A WALL! Are you mad, Alexandra? Didn't it occur to you to say that your sister was seriously injured and couldn't walk? Couldn't you have said, "Please help us," like a normal human being?'

When my sister blows her top, she does it in a spectacular way. First she screams and shakes her head from side to side, then she says things like, '*I don't believe you said that. That is so stupid. How could you?*'

I've heard it all before. But that day was worse than usual. I had to wait a long time until she'd calmed down and only when she'd stopped shouting did I tell her what I'd seen.

'One of them was a great thug with a vicious dog,' I said. 'He was huge – massive with really mean eyes and a big belly. I bet he could kill a rat with his little finger. Squash it . . . like that!'

'Gross.'

'The other one looked like Dracula with his dead pale face and the black uniform. He was pure evil.'

'You're exaggerating.'

'I'm not! I heard him say he was pleased that Grandad's cottage was destroyed *and* he thought Grandad was in it.'

'No! I don't believe it!'

'Honest. They talked as if they'd done it themselves.'

'You probably didn't hear right. The storm did the damage.'

'What they said was that we were in the target zone. Those were the words they used and that sounds like war talk to me.'

It took some time for Kirstie to take me seriously.

'I see why you hid behind the wall,' she said. 'So what do we do now?'

'We wait here till Dad gets back. He said he'd catch the last ferry.'

'No. I can't stay in this hole any longer, Ally. I'll go up those steps on my bottom if I have to. I know it'll take ages but it's the only way.'

I tried arguing, but she wouldn't listen, so I helped her across the cellar. She sat on the first step and slowly pushed herself up to the next one with her good leg.

It took forever but when Kirstie finally reached the top, she stared open-mouthed at what she saw. 'Oh my God, Ally. I can't believe it. This is worse than I thought.'

The wind was blowing among the wreckage, through the remains of the kitchen, scattering newspapers and magazines, sending them flapping into the fields like weird birds. Only Lizzie was unfazed by the catastrophe. She was just glad to be above ground again – and went wild, leaping among the rubble, stirring up dust and somehow making us laugh.

Afterwards, Kirstie said, 'I'm desperate for the loo. Where is it?' – which was typical of my sister. She always needs to go to the toilet at the most inconsiderate times.

'It's over there where it always was,' I said, pointing to a mound of broken brick that had once been a wall. 'But it's smashed to pieces.'

'I've got to go. I've been hanging on for ages.'

I went over to the corner and shifted the remains of the loo door so that it made a small cubicle. 'This area can be for your personal use, madam.'

She nodded. 'Not funny. But I suppose it'll keep the smells in one place.' And she began to shuffle towards it. 'I'll be glad when Dad gets back to sort all this out. We can't be putting up with it for long.'

When she finally reached the spot, she called out that she was having problems with her jeans. 'I can't undo the zip,' she yelled. Then, 'Oh no, I can't get them down.' Honestly! Fuss. Fuss. Fuss. She makes a fuss about everything.

Back in the kitchen, the fridge was hardly damaged. There was food inside and I was starving so I took things out – ice cream (slightly melted), chicken, a couple of tomatoes and a carton of orange juice – and I found a towel in a drawer and spread it on the small piece of floor that was free of rubble.

Kirstie emerged from the loo.

'I'm making us a picnic,' I said. 'It won't be as good as Mrs Cameron's tea, but it's not bad.'

Kirstie clapped her hands to her cheeks. 'Mrs Cameron! Oh no, I'd forgotten. Ally, don't you think you should go across to the farm and tell them what's happened? They could help us.'

'Good idea,' I said, biting into the chicken.

'I'll be here if Dad comes back.'

'What time do you make it? My watch has stopped.'

Kirstie looked at hers and frowned. 'Mine's stopped, too.' She shook her wrist but the watch showed no signs of life. 'It stopped at half past two. Probably when that rubble fell on top of me.'

'No. Mine stopped at exactly the same time.'

'So what time do you think it is now?'

'According to my stomach, it's around tea time. The Camerons will be wondering why we haven't gone over there.'

I took a glug out of the carton of orange and stood up. 'Right then, I'm off. You'll be OK, won't you?'

'Sure. Just get back as soon as you can, eh?'

I stumbled through the rubble of the kitchen to the outside. It must have been later than we thought because the daylight was already fading. I would have to hurry.

But I was no more than a hundred metres from the cottage when darkness fell so completely that it was as if a black cloth had been thrown over the earth. I didn't want to be alone out there on my own and I couldn't face the two-mile walk across the fields. No way. I would have to go back.

Chapter Six

I knew Kirstie would be terrified, alone and in sudden darkness. I got back as soon as I could.

'Kirstie!' I shouted as I stumbled into the ruined cottage. 'Don't panic. I'm here.'

'Ally!' she called out. 'It's so scary with no lights.' I soon felt my way across the debris to where she was sitting. 'Isn't there a torch anywhere?'

I didn't know of a torch but I knew Grandad kept candles and matches in the cupboard under the sink – in case of power cuts, of course. I felt my way across the kitchen and found them, undamaged. I lit a candle and held it high above my head. The devastation around us looked far worse in the eerie light of the little flame. But I could see the mattress off my bed, ripped and covered in dust, over in the corner. And a chest of drawers, which had smashed as it fell through the ceiling, had spewed out all my clothes. These things could be really useful.

'I'll get you a sweater, Kirst,' I said, scrambling over broken floorboards towards the chest of drawers. 'It's getting pretty cold.'

'Too right,' she moaned. 'If it gets any colder, I'll

freeze to death. My nose must be blue already. It feels like an icicle.'

I could tell she was getting depressed – what with the pain of her foot and everything.

'Think of it as an adventure, sis,' I said as I rummaged among the heap of clothes. 'How many kids will have this kind of summer holiday? The best they'll have will be a week at Disney World. Wait till we get back to school and tell everybody, eh? House collapses. Kids struggle to survive. You could write a brilliant book about it.'

I found my favourite sweater (hurray) and some old ones which I gave to Kirstie.

We put on as many layers as we could, and then Kirstie asked if I could find something for her foot. 'Get a sheet or a towel, Ally. Strapping it tight might help reduce the swelling.'

'It'll hurt.'

'I'll manage.'

I pulled the sheet off the mattress and she tore it into strips.

'Are you sure this is the right thing to do, Kirstie?'

'Yes, Mum showed me once. I wanted to be a nurse like her, when I was younger. I loved that kind of stuff.'

'Now you want to write books,' I said as I began to wrap the bandage round the lower part of her leg. She gritted her teeth but didn't make a sound until I had finished, then she let out a long, agonising groan and curled herself up, wrapping her arms round her body, trying to rock away the pain.

While she recovered, I somehow managed to drag the mattress across the rubble and over to the wall.

'Lie on this, Kirstie. It's a bit dusty but it's comfy and we've got a duvet. How lucky is that, eh?' That cheered her up.

By the light of the candle, she rolled onto the mattress and pulled the duvet up to her chin. I threw myself down next to her and Lizzie jumped on after me.

'She'll help to keep us warm.'

'Just as long as she stays away from my foot.'

So the three of us lay on the mattress – two under the duvet and one on top. As a matter of fact, I was enjoying myself. It was like camping out without any adults around spying on you.

'It's fantastic to be warm, don't you think?'

'Yes. Pity the duvet doesn't cover my head. I think my ears will drop off with the cold.'

'I can solve that problem, my lady. I have something over in one of the drawers.'

'You mean your woolly hats?'

'No. My knickers. They'll do the job in an emergency.'

'I am NOT wearing your knickers on my head. No way. What a stupid idea.'

But I was already rummaging in the heap of clothes. 'It's not stupid. Knickers are just the right size. But if you'd rather freeze...'

'Couldn't I have a T-shirt?'

I came back with a bundle of things. 'Take your pick. Why worry about what you'll look like? I'm not going to take a photo.'

Kirstie tried a T-shirt on her head but it was too big and it flopped about and wouldn't stay in place. So she gave in and pulled on a pair of spotted pants instead.

'Better?'

'Better.'

We lay down again and waited, listening for Dad. We still hoped he would come and we talked to keep away the scary thoughts that crept into our heads.

'I bet I know what's happened.'

'What?'

'I bet that guy who runs the ferry...'

'Robbie Roberts?'

'Yeah. I bet he went home when the thunder-storm started. I can just hear him, "Ah well, I'm no running the ferry in weather like this. Who would expect a body to do that, eh? I'm away to have ma supper."'

Kirstie laughed at my impersonation – which was pretty good. (If I don't become a computer expert like Dad, I might have my own TV show impersonating famous people. I'll think about it.)

'You're probably right,' Kirstie said. 'There won't be a ferry tonight so Dad won't be back until morning. He'll expect us to be over at the farm.'

For once, my sister made sense.

'We should get some sleep. Worrying about it won't help, will it?'

I blew out the candle and pulled the duvet up to my chin. Without any light, it was difficult to tell whether my eyes were open or shut – the blackness of that night was so dense. And there was no sound at all except for the wind blowing through gaps where there had once been windows and walls. There were no owls hooting. No sheep bleating. We lay there feeling as if we were the only people alive on the planet and every other creature had been wiped from the face of the earth.

35

Until the noise came.

Kirstie lifted herself onto her elbows and said, 'What's that?'

I sat up, too, and listened. It came again. It was coming from over the hill.

'I don't know. I'll go outside and see if I can find out.'

I lit the candle and clambered through the ruins of the cottage. But the wind soon blew out the candle and I stood outside in the black night and waited and listened.

'Can you hear anything?' Kirstie called.

'Not a thing. Whatever it was, I think it's gone.'

I was about to go back to the comfort of the mattress when the noise came again. A screaming that wasn't human. A banging. It was a good distance away and I stood there listening until it stopped.

'What was it?' Kirstie asked.

'An animal, for sure, and I think it's trapped. It sounded terrified.'

'Maybe a fox was after it.'

'No. It's a big animal. Maybe a horse.'

'Don't be daft. Where could a horse get trapped?'

I climbed back onto the mattress. We lay there, wide awake, until Kirstie spoke.

'This is a weird night, Ally. I've never known such blackness. Supposing tomorrow morning...'

'What?'

'...supposing it doesn't get light. What then?'

Chapter Seven

My sister was being ridiculous. The sun rose the following day as it had done for millions of years before and flooded the island with sunshine.

I sat up in bed feeling great. 'Dad will be over on the first ferry. You wait and see. No probs.'

Kirstie opened her eyes. 'No problems?' You've got to be joking! The cottage is a wreck. I've broken my ankle. Apart from that, I suppose everything is perfect. Silly me for thinking we were in a mess.'

I jumped off the mattress. 'You know, Kirstie, you can be very negative. You always look on the black side. Think positive thoughts, that's my advice.'

'I can think positively when I need to. For one – you look positively ridiculous with those knickers on your head.'

She had a point. I snatched them off and threw them at her and she threw them back and a knickers fight followed. Lizzie dashed from one to the other, barking and making the whole game more frantic and when one pair of pants finally landed in Kirstie's private toilet area, we fell about laughing.

'Yuk. You won't be wearing that pair again, sis.'

I decided we should have breakfast and went to look in the fridge. 'Do you think this cheese will be OK? And what about the milk?'

The electricity had been off for less than twenty-four hours, so we thought that everything should be fine. We sniffed the milk just to make sure. It was definitely OK. I even found cupboards with a few unbroken bowls and mugs and some packets of cereal and biscuits.

'A feast!' I said, putting the food on the mattress. 'We can survive for days with what's in those cupboards. We'll be like Robinson Crusoe on his desert island.'

'Stop acting like a silly kid. We won't have to survive. Dad will be coming this morning.'

I shrugged and poured some cereal for myself and some for Lizzie and topped them with milk. 'When we've had breakfast, I'm going to the farm.'

'I'm coming too.'

My mouth was full of Shreddies so I had to shake my head violently. Honestly! How could she walk to the farm with that ankle? Did she think she was Superwoman?

But my sister is stubborn.

'I'm not staying by myself. It's not likely Dad

will be here in the next half hour. Anyway, I'll write a note for him.'

I argued but it was no good.

'Now *you're* being negative. I think I could do it.'

'How?'

'If you got me a stick to lean on, I could manage. The pain's not so bad now and I'm sure the swelling's gone down since we bandaged it.'

In the end, I gave in and went to find a suitable branch to use as a crutch. There was a tree near the cottage – a gnarled old rowan which had been uprooted in the storm. Broken branches were scattered everywhere and I soon found one with a fork at the top which was perfect. Then we wrapped a towel round the top part to stop it digging into Kirstie's armpit. Done. Fixed. Finished.

'That's great,' she said. 'Look, I can walk with it.'

Well, not exactly. She could hop. She could hobble. She could shuffle. But she couldn't really walk.

We wrote a note for Dad telling him where we'd gone, and we left it on the path held down with a stone. Then we set off. With a bit of help, Kirstie managed to manoeuvre through the rubble, keeping her injured foot off the ground and using the crutch to support her. But when she looked across the fields, she realised that the walk to the Camerons' farm would be impossible for her.

'What can I do, Ally? I really, really want to go with you.'

I hadn't a clue what to do until I saw the broken pieces of the front door lying on the ground.

'That's big enough to make a sort-of sledge. I could tie some rope on the handle and pull you.'

'Have we got some rope?'

'In the shed, I think.'

I went and found some good strong rope which was just the thing. I pushed it through a knothole in the wood and made a handle to pull it with.

'Right. Get on, Kirst, and we'll see if it works.'

With some difficulty, she managed to climb onto the makeshift sledge and sit down. Then we all set off – with Lizzie running round us, barking. I gripped the rope and pulled the sledge over the grass in the direction of the farm. At first it moved easily but as the land began to rise towards the hill, it became more difficult and I grunted from the exertion.

'I'll see if my crutch will help,' Kirstie called and she started to use it rather like the paddle in a boat,

41

pushing into the ground and propelling the sledge forward.

'Thanks,' I panted. 'That's great.'

Even with the help of the crutch, getting to the top of the hill was difficult. It was hard work for me and uncomfortable for Kirstie, lurching from side to side over the rough ground.

By the time we reached the top we were both gasping. But we were not prepared for what we saw. Down below in the valley, the Camerons' farmhouse was totally destroyed. Wiped out. We couldn't move, we were so shocked by the devastation.

'The whole place is just a pile of stones,' I said.

'The Camerons must be under all that,' said Kirstie. 'Oh, Ally. It's terrible. They couldn't have survived.'

'How do you know? They might be still alive. We're still alive, aren't we? I'm not staying here. I'm going to look.'

I went running down the hill with Lizzie at my heels, leaving Kirstie at the top. But she yelled after me, 'You're not going without me. I'm coming.'

I turned to look and saw her dig the crutch into the ground and push so that the sledge began to slide down the slope. Crazy girl! The hill was steep.

Before long the sledge was out of control and racing ahead. It was whizzing along and there was no chance of stopping it. I only hoped that Kirstie could hang on.

Chapter Eight

When the sledge reached the bottom, it came to a halt in a patch of thick mud – which was OK as it was nice and soft – although Kirstie wasn't impressed by the mess of it all and I had to give her a hand to pull her out.

'Keep Lizzie with you,' I said. 'I'll go and look round. Maybe I'll find them.'

I walked around the back of the ruined farmhouse to the yard where the barns and pigsties were. These buildings had suffered less damage than the farmhouse but, even so, they were wrecked and there was no sign of the pigs or chickens – they must have fled during the storm. The whole place was deserted. There was nothing here.

I was about to go back to Kirstie when I saw something over by the pigsties and so I ran towards it. As I got nearer, I realised there was a man lying on the ground. It was Mr Cameron! He must have been injured.

I raced across to him shouting, 'Mr Cameron! It's Ally. Are you all right?'

He was lying in the dirt face down and when I reached him, I leaned over and touched his shoulder. 'Mr Cameron. It's Alexandra, Mr Cameron.' He didn't move. He must be unconscious, I thought. There was no one to help. I tried to think back to my first aid and I gripped his arm with one hand and his shoulder with the other and rolled him onto his back. He was heavy but I managed it.

As soon as I saw his face, I knew that he wasn't unconscious. A trickle of dried blood spread from his mouth, his eyes were wide open and fixed with a terrified stare. His skin was ash grey and there was no doubt about it. He was dead.

I screamed and snatched my hand away, horrified.

'Kirstie!' I shouted, as I ran back sobbing. 'I've seen Mr Cameron! I've seen him. He's dead! He's dead!'

Kirstie was just as upset as I was and it took us time to calm down. When we did, we decided it was pointless looking any more. We wanted to go back. But Lizzie suddenly broke free from Kirstie's grip and ran in the direction of the yard. I was worried she was heading for Mr Cameron's body – maybe she had smelled it – but no, she ran beyond the yard, barking and barking.

Then we heard what she must have heard. The wild terrified neighing of a horse. Trapped and scared witless, beating its hooves against a door.

'That was the noise. Last night. Remember, Ally? He must be in a stable.'

The stable was a distance from the yard and was much older than the farm and had thick, thick walls. Part of the roof had been ripped away but the walls had survived the storm.

'I can't bear to hear him, Ally. He sounds so frightened. If we can't do anything for the Camerons, we can get him out.'

'We'll have to go past the body, Kirst. Are you all right with that?'

She nodded unconvincingly, grasped her crutch and began to hobble across the yard. Neither of us dared look over to Mr Cameron as we passed. We kept our eyes fixed on the stable door.

'I'll talk to the horse and calm him down. You can open the door and fetch him out, Ally.'

'No way. As soon as you open that door, he'll bolt.'

'Don't be silly. Go and find some water. Fill a bucket or whatever's handy. He's sure to be thirsty.'

The tap was by the pigsties. I walked across the yard holding my chin up and staring straight ahead of me so I needn't look at the body. But even though I didn't look, I still felt sick and I began to shake. I managed to fill an old black bucket then I hurried back to Kirstie.

She was leaning against the stable wall, talking to the horse through the door. Kirstie's a pain most of the time but she's brilliant with horses. Ever since she was eight, she's had riding lessons and she's been able to communicate with them. She can soothe them when they're frightened or even when they're ill. She's amazing. Everybody says so.

I had only been away for a few minutes but, in that time, the horse was calmer and was no longer whinnying. I could still hear him pawing the ground though – but somehow he didn't sound so frightened.

'Shall we open the door, Kirst?'

'Not yet. Give me a bit longer.'

She continued to talk slowly and soothingly and then she surprised me by starting to sing. My sister has a rubbish singing voice – I'd always told her so – but here she was calming a frantic horse with a lullaby. It was magic. There was no more stamping or snorting. The horse was calm. I was gobsmacked by what she had done.

She unbolted the door and I pulled it open – slowly, slowly. Then, as the light flooded into the stable, we saw the horse for the first time. Huge and brown with a striking white blaze on his nose. Still singing, Kirstie held out her hand as if to stroke him. The horse backed away, tossing his head but she hopped forward until she could touch his nose. I felt sick. The horse could have knocked her over in a flash. She had one good leg and a stick, that's all. She wouldn't stand a chance.

Wobbling a little, Kirstie reached out to take a head collar that was hanging on the wall. The horse made no sound. Then, still singing, she slipped it on over his head as gently as you like and fastened the lead rope, pausing only to say, 'Take him, Ally,' and passing the rope over to me. I took it and led the horse through the door and into the open air.

'Fantastic, Kirst! Brilliant. Absolutely brilliant!'

'Shhh. Quiet, Ally. You'll freak him out. Stay calm and let him drink the water.'

We stood nearby while he emptied the bucket I had carried from the yard.

'We'll have to take him with us,' Kirstie insisted. She was right. There was no one here to look after him and there was plenty of good grass near the cottage.

In fact, the horse was a great solution to our problem. Kirstie could ride him. It would have taken forever to pull her up the hill on the sledge.

I made a cradle with my hands and she put her good foot into it and pushed herself up so that she flopped forward across the horse's back. She lay there for a moment or two whispering gently into his ear then she pivoted around, swinging her injured foot across to the other side. So she was able to sit upright and she was ready to ride.

'You lead the horse and bring my stick, will you, Ally?'

As we walked on past the pile of stones that had been the farmhouse, neither of us spoke. I guess we were both thinking about the Camerons. One lay dead in the yard and the other was probably buried under the stones. We would never see them again.

Chapter Nine

When we got back to the cottage, there was still no sign of Dad. The note was there as we had left it, trapped under the stone, flapping at the corners. No one had touched it.

Kirstie went into one of her depressed phases and flopped down on the mattress.

'Cheer up,' I said.

She just sneered at me. 'You are *so annoying*. Go away.'

'Don't get ratty with me, sis. There's no point in hanging around looking miserable. We've got to do something.'

'Like what?'

'We'll go down to the village. There'll be somebody who knows what's happened. I bet there's a simple explanation.'

She just shook her head and didn't say anything.

'Think about it,' I said. 'The ferry could have blown away in the storm. Probably all the boats for miles around have got swept out to sea...or sunk. It's not Dad's fault that he's stuck on the mainland, is it?'

Kirstie didn't seem to take in my logic. She was more concerned with her ankle. She just kept looking at it.

'This is worse than when I woke up. The pain is awful. I'm not sure I can come to the harbour.' She leaned forward and touched it. 'It's swelling. I think going to the farm made it worse.'

'Yeah. You're supposed to keep your foot up if it's swollen.'

'What I need is a doctor and the nearest one is in Balfour. How do I get there if there's no ferry?'

'Never fear. Ally's here,' I said and knelt down and began to unwind the bandage from round her foot. 'I'll put a poultice on it. I've seen Mum do it loads of times. It's easy. You'll be fit as a flea in no time.'

Before the car accident, Mum had been interested in herbal remedies. She said they were often more effective than pills the doctor prescribed. Grandad had herbs in his garden so there must be some out there. The snag was, herbs all looked the same to me – just leaves with no names. But Kirstie didn't need to know that. I could convince her I was an expert. Easy.

I looked around outside and found what I thought were herbs. Some had withered and died but others looked good. There was a big bushy thing that smelled nice and a taller one with thin leaves like needles. I took a handful of each for good luck.

'What are you going to do with those?' she said when I took them inside.

'You just relax,' I said and went over to the kitchen cupboard and fetched a plastic bowl. I shredded the leaves, added a few drops of water and squished it with my hands until it turned into a green slime like seaweed.

'You're not putting that on my leg, are you?'

I wasn't offended. She just didn't appreciate my talent.

'Leave it to Doctor Dunbar. This poultice has healing properties. It's one of Mum's secret recipes.'

In spite of her complaints, I put the mixture on her ankle and wrapped the bandage on top. The liquid oozed through the bandage of course and turned it green – but never mind.

'Disgusting colour,' Kirstie complained. Then as she felt the cool on her ankle, she said, 'Oh thanks, Ally. It's feeling better already.'

See? The power of healing.

I insisted that she lay down with her foot higher than her head. (I knew this from a hospital soap on the telly.) Then I told her to close her eyes. I was hoping she would fall asleep and that would give me time to slip down to the ferry to find out when the next one was due. But it didn't happen. She didn't fall asleep and after half an hour, she said her foot had stopped throbbing and she was ready to go.

'I'll ride on the horse. I don't want to stay here if I don't have to.'

'Good old Dobbin,' I said. I had secretly given the horse this great traditional name.

'Dobbin!' Kirstie nearly choked. She didn't like my choice – she was sentimental about horses. 'He's probably got a beautiful name. Pegasus or Ulysses.'

'No. Never. Too flashy. I prefer Dobbin. A good solid reliable name. Are you coming or what?'

Dobbin (as he was called from then on) was tied to the uprooted tree, so I undid the rope and led him with Kirstie sitting astride, up to the narrow lane that led down to the village. It was two miles away but I reckoned we could be there in half an hour. What we hoped to see was the ferry bringing Dad from the mainland. Now that would be something!

Caitlin was a small harbour village – no more than a post office and a row of fishermen's cottages. Not that there were any fishermen left. The waters round the island were so polluted that fish didn't swim there any more. Who could blame them? I wouldn't swim in it either.

We had almost reached the village when we heard the sound of a noisy engine and a large vehicle flashed past the bottom of the lane travelling along the harbour road.

'People!' Kirstie yelled. 'Get a move on, Ally, before they disappear.'

What my dim sister hadn't noticed was that this wasn't any old car or four-wheel drive. This was a military vehicle. An APC – an armoured military personnel carrier. Some people would call it a tank, but it isn't. This one was unusual because it was painted black and there was a silver flash of lightning painted on the side. Alarm bells started ringing for me.

I pulled on Dobbin's rope. 'Stop, Kirstie. Wait here,' I said. 'I want to be sure who these people are.'

'Why?'

'Because they might be connected with the two men who came up to the cottage yesterday.'

'And they might not be. For goodness sake, we've got to talk to them. Get some help.'

It took a while but I finally persuaded her to stay put while I ran to the bottom of the lane. I didn't want to be seen until I was sure everything was OK, so when I reached the corner, I dropped to my hands and knees. I kept my head close to the ground and I peeped down the harbour road. What I saw was the large black vehicle parked near the ferry station. Six men, all in the same black uniforms, climbed out and stood in a group looking at a map. I recognised one as the Sumo Wrestler and he was holding thea map. The tallest of the group was pointing to it and this was Dracula himself.

While I was watching, my eyes drifted towards the row of cottages. I wish I hadn't looked. Just like Grandad's cottage and the Camerons' farm, they had been reduced to a heap of stone. The village looked like a battle zone. It just didn't exist.

Dracula looked up from the map and pointed across to Balfour, sweeping his hand from right to left as if picking out landmarks. The men around him seemed to be listening to instructions as they fixed their eyes on the mainland.

What happened next was unexpected and terrifying.

Lizzie had stayed behind with Kirstie but before I

realised what was happening, she was racing down the lane towards me. Suddenly, she stopped, growled softly and I saw her hackles rise. She had sensed something was wrong. Had she smelled the men? Had she heard them? Before I could grab her, she hared past me and turned the corner, barking ferociously and heading towards the men in black uniforms. They turned to look. Some of them burst out laughing when they saw her. Some of them called, 'Here boy!'

But one of them didn't.

It was Dracula who pulled a gun from its holster, raised it in both hands and aimed it at Lizzie.

Then he fired.

Chapter Ten

I sunk my head in my hands, shaking with the horror of it, not wanting to see. When I did look up, the men had folded their map and were climbing back into the APC. But there was no sign of Lizzie – except for dark patches splattered on the tarmac which looked sickeningly like blood.

I raced up the lane to where Kirstie was still waiting, wide-eyed with fright. 'What happened, Ally? I heard the shot. Who was firing?' Then she saw that the dog wasn't with me. 'Where's Lizzie?'

I felt sick with fear and anger.

'Now will you believe me? Those men are evil. They shot her, that's what. She ran towards them and they shot her. What kind of people shoot a dog?'

Kirstie's face crumpled and she covered her cheeks as tears began to flow. I tried to make her feel better but I didn't feel so good myself. I had to tell her about the village, too. It seemed that everywhere around us had been destroyed in the storm. Everything.

When we heard the engine of the APC start up, we pulled Dobbin into the hedgerow to hide as best we could – just in case they should come this way. We heard them pass the bottom of the lane, heading back the way they had come. I don't think anyone glanced up the lane as they went by – or, if they did, they didn't see us. They were gone.

It was Kirstie's idea to use the public call box to contact Dad on his mobile. The storm hadn't touched the one on the seafront. It was one of those really old red phone boxes they used to have before everybody had mobiles. It was standing proud and solid amidst the ruins of the village. Dad said they kept the phone boxes for emergencies. Well, this was an emergency all right.

'We'll need coins,' Kirstie said.

I felt in my pockets but I hadn't got any and neither had she. I turned to look at the pile of rubble where the post office had been. There was just a chance I could find the till. It was a long shot but I'd give it a go.

The till must have been well buried. All I could see among the stone was the wrecked counter and some stuff off the shelves in the shop. Bottles of toilet cleaner and air freshener were no good to me at this minute. I carried on looking for money and had almost given up the search, when I heard a noise some way away. It was a soft, pitiful whine – it was Lizzie. I knew it! Amazed and delighted, I yelled, 'Lizzie. Hold on, girl. I'm coming,' and clambered across the wreckage of the shop, looking among the rubble, until I found her. She was lying limp and helpless, her tongue lolling from her mouth as she panted, her coat soaked in blood.

Gently, I lifted her and struggled back to Kirstie who was overjoyed to see that she was still alive. She slid off Dobbin and held out her arms to take her.

'Oh Lizzie. Lizzie!' she said. 'We'll take care of you. Oh, you poor thing.'

The bullet had ripped the flesh at the top of her front leg. It was a miracle that it hadn't struck her chest – that would have killed her for sure. What we needed to do now was to clean the wound.

'I'll see what I can find in the post office. There's all kinds of stuff lying in the rubble.'

I soon found a bottle of water and took it back to Kirstie, who bathed the wound and used some of her own bandage to strap Lizzie's leg.

For some time we were so caught up with Lizzie's problems, that we forgot our own. But when we had done what we could for her, we began to think about what our next move should be.

'There's no one around here to help,' Kirstie said. 'What do we do? We can't ring Dad without money.'

As if a light bulb had switched on in my brain, I realised that we were being really stupid. It cost nothing to call the police. We just had to dial 999. I went over to the call box and opened the door. I lifted the receiver and tapped out the number, but there was no ringing tone. I put the receiver down and tried again. Nothing. I tried four times but it was useless.

'This phone's broken. I expect the line's down. Just let's go, Kirstie. Those men could come back. Come on. Get back on Dobbin and let's get out of here.'

She stood there, holding Lizzie, staring down the street.

'That's Robbie Roberts' car. Look! Over there by the harbour wall.'

The storm hadn't damaged the wall, which was a couple of metres thick, and the wall had protected the car.

'So it's Robbie's car. So what?'

'I could drive it, that's what. I could take us across the island, over to Tarbay. There'll be people there.'

'Are you mad? You can't drive! You haven't got a licence! You haven't got insurance!'

60

She looked at me as if I was something that had crawled out of the ground. 'Think, Alexandra. Do you see a policeman waiting to arrest me? Do you see anyone wanting to check my licence?'

I hate my sister sometimes.

'But what about keys to start the engine?'

She gave me one of her smarmy self-satisfied smiles. 'Robbie always leaves them in the ignition. There's nobody on Shairn who would steal it, is there?'

Kirstie handed Lizzie to me, climbed onto Dobbin and together we headed to the harbour. Earlier in the year, Dad had given Kirstie a couple of driving lessons on the old airfield near our house. It was just for fun. She couldn't apply for her driving licence for years.

'Actually, there's nothing to it,' she said smugly as we reached the car. She slid off Dobbin's back, hobbled across and reached for the door handle.

That was when we saw Robbie Roberts sitting in the driver's seat. It was the answer to our prayers. Someone to help us. He knew this island better than anyone.

'Robbie!' Kirstie squealed and opened the door.

Slowly, Robbie fell sideways, his eyes open and

terrified, his skin white and bloodless. Just like Mr Cameron. Robbie Roberts was dead.

Kirstie freaked out. She screamed over and over again. She was hysterical. Out of control. I put Lizzie on the ground, then took Kirstie and sat her on the harbour wall.

'OK,' I said when she had calmed down. 'Let's be practical here. This car's no use to Robbie now, right?

'No.'

'But it'll get us to safety...'

'Yes.'

'...once we've moved him out of the driver's seat.'

That freaked her even more. 'I can't. I can't. I won't touch him. He's dead! No, no, no, Ally. I'm not touching a dead body.'

She started crying again so I stood up and just got on with it. There was nothing else I could do if we were going to get across the island. While Kirstie wailed, I shut my eyes tight and put my hands under Robbie's armpits and tugged him from behind the wheel. He was heavy and stiff. Not like a person at all. I pretended he was one of those dummies you see in shop windows. That made it easier for me. His foot was trapped in the pedals but, bit by bit, I jiggled and pulled him free and his legs came out. I dragged him clear of the car and dropped him onto the ground. Then I opened the door and lifted Lizzie onto the back seat. There was a wool blanket spread across it so she would be comfortable there.

'Right,' I called to Kirstie when I had finished. 'We're ready for off.'

'There is no way I'm getting in that car,' Kirstie screamed. 'No way! I'm not sitting in a dead man's seat.'

'How else will we get to Tarbay? Want to stay here and wait for the Men in Black?'

She knew we had no choice. I took my sweater off and covered the driver's seat with it and Kirstie finally agreed to get in.

'You've only got one good foot, Kirstie. How are you going to change gear?'

'You'll have to do that.'

She pointed down to a pedal on the floor of the car. 'Reach over with your right foot. Can you push it down?'

It was difficult, but I managed.

'Every time I say NOW, Ally, you have to press

the pedal as hard as you can while I change gear. Then I press the accelerator with my right foot and we take off. OK? We'll be out of this horrible place in no time.'

'OK, Kirst. Keep your fingers crossed. Let's go.'

Chapter Eleven

Kirstie turned the key in the ignition but the car wouldn't start.

'You must be doing it wrong!' I said.

'I'm not,' she said. 'Haven't I seen Dad start the car a thousand times?'

She tried again and again but there was no sound of life in the engine.

We checked the petrol.

OK.

We even tried looking under the bonnet – that's what everybody does. We couldn't see anything wrong and there didn't seem to be anything missing. It looked fine.

It just wouldn't start.

'Sea water. Rain water. It could be anything.'

'There was lots of thunder yesterday so there was probably lightning, too, and that might have taken out the electrics – maybe.'

We agreed there was no point in hanging around. The men in black might come back. What if they did? Where could we hide? The thought of it was too frightening. Somehow, we had to get over to

Tarbay and tell someone what had happened in our village. It was the only thing to do.

'So you ride Dobbin and I walk,' I said.

'It'll take hours,' Kirstie replied. 'We'll need food to take with us.'

I ran back to the other end of the harbour and scrabbled among the ruins of the shop for anything I could find – I picked up a box of cheese triangles, some sandwiches in a squashed plastic box and two dented cans of Coke. Not a feast – but it was something, at least.

Then I wrapped Lizzie in the blanket from the car and tied it round Kirstie's waist. That way she could ride on Dobbin. She was too heavy to carry and too weak to walk.

Once we had organised ourselves, we took the road that headed north out of the village. The men in the APC had gone south. We wanted to get as far from them as we could. But it turned out to be more difficult than we thought. Once we had left the village, the road became a narrow track, steep and stony, and we found the going hard and really slow. Three miles on, it levelled out, thank goodness, and we moved faster. The path hugged the coastline and we had a fantastic view of a side of the island I had never seen before. Whenever we came to visit Grandad, we had always explored the side near to the cottage. This was the north of the island and it was rugged and wild. The path we were following sometimes shifted beneath our feet making it difficult to get a firm foothold. Sometimes it swung close to the cliff edge where the land fell away in a sheer drop to the water below. I led Dobbin slowly and carefully, talking to him all the time while Kirstie shut her eyes and refused to look until we had passed the danger zone.

During our journey, we only saw one sign of life. That was a motorboat anchored in a small cove.

'There must be people around. There must be!' Kirstie insisted.

We stood and shouted from the cliff top but the wind took our voices away and no one came – and so we set off again.

As we continued, the path almost disappeared and there was one spot where Dobbin stumbled on some loose stones. It was time to stop and re-think. I helped Kirstie down and she sat on a boulder by the edge of the road.

'I can't go much further. It's getting worse. I don't think anyone comes up here. Ever.'

'Grandad said there used to be a road right round the island but nobody used it. The people who lived in Tarbay weren't keen to spend good money on repairing it.'

'That explains it.'

'Yes.'

'But how do they get to Tarbay now?'

'There's supposed to be a road on the other side of the island. I've seen it on a map, that's all.'

'We should have gone the other way.'

'And passed the Men in Black? No thank you.'

'Maybe it's impossible this way. Look – the sun's sinking already. We'll never make it before dark. It's hopeless, Ally. Let's turn back.'

By then, she was in one of her Gloom and Doom moods. But not me.

'If I run to the top of that slope, Kirstie, I might be able to see something. It might be good news.'

I set off on foot while Dobbin rested and Kirstie sat with Lizzie, who was brighter now and trying to hobble around. As I climbed up to a craggy ridge, a bitter wind sprang up, whipping at my face and chilling me to the bone. I scrambled on my hands and knees over the crumbly crag to reach the top. There I saw the island spread out in front of me like a three-dimensional map and, on the far side, I could make out a group of cottages – Tarbay – clinging to the shore, pink-tinted in the sun. But it was a long way off.

I hurried back down the hill to Kirstie. 'We won't make it today,' I said, trying to get my breath back. 'Tarbay is miles off.'

'Do we go back to the village?'

'Too dangerous.'

'Then what?'

'I saw an old bothy about a mile away. We could stay there and go on in the morning. It's better than nothing.'

Last night, we had slept in the wreck of Grandad's cottage. The bothy couldn't be worse than that. These stone huts were built in remote parts of Scotland for travellers who might need shelter for the night. Well, we were travellers and we certainly needed shelter.

It seemed to take forever but, somehow, we managed to cover that mile in spite of the biting wind. When the path got really difficult, Kirstie had to get off Dobbin, hold onto my shoulder and hobble along as best she could. But we were in for a nice surprise. What I had thought was a stone hut turned out to be something much better. It was an old chapel – though I had no idea why anyone would want to build a chapel miles from anywhere, even a small one. It was a piece of luck for us. The roof was sound and we would be out of the wind with room for us all, Kirstie, Dobbin, Lizzie and me.

'We've got one blanket, at least,' Kirstie said as we reached the door. 'I wish we'd got a sleeping bag or something. If it's another night like last night, we'll freeze to death.'

'Last night was creepy after the storm. But it's not going to happen again, right?'

We opened the door and looked into the little chapel. It was black as pitch.

'You go in first, Ally. Check for rats and things. You know I can't stand anything like that.'

There was only one window and that didn't help much because the light was fading – but I went in and waited till my eyes became adjusted to the dark. Then I walked to the far end, looking around as I went, wishing I'd thought to bring the candle with me. But when we set out that morning, we weren't expecting to trek across the island, were we?

There was a stone floor covered in soil and bits of dead grass and stuff that must have blown under the door and a sack of cattle feed – probably left by a farmer who kept animals on the hillside. But there wasn't much else. I was about to go back to Kirstie, when I heard something behind me. I stood still and listened. What I heard was breathing. There was no doubt about it. My skin began to prickle and my heart thumped against my ribs. Slowly, I turned to look over my shoulder. In the far corner, something moved and I knew for sure that I was not alone.

Chapter Twelve

I stood there in the dim light of the chapel as if I were frozen to the spot. I was petrified. Something – or someone – was there. But what should I do? I couldn't phone the police or send for a SWAT team, could I? What if it was a criminal hiding in the chapel? What if it was a bear crouching, waiting to spring?

I decided to leg it.

Just as I turned to go there was a terrible scream. 'AAAAAAAAAAAGHHHHHHHHHHHHHH!!!! !!!!!!!!'

Then a voice:

'WHO ARE YOU? LEAVE ME ALONE! GO AWAY, I WON'T TELL YOU ANYTHING!'

Kirstie heard the screaming and she started yelling, too. 'ALLY! WHAT'S HAPPENING? WHAT'S HAPPENING? COME OUT QUICK!'

I was amazed to see Lizzie come shooting through the door on three legs, barking and growling. All the noise practically split my head open and I clapped my hands over my ears.

'STOP IT!' I yelled over the din and everything

went quiet – even our dog who came and stood by me.

In that moment, I admit that I was stuck for something to say. So I just called out, 'Hello! Can I help you?'

There was no reply so I tried again. 'Hello?'

This time a voice said, 'Who are you?'

Feeling nervous, I replied, 'I'm Alexandra Dunbar. Who are you?'

'I need to know what you're doing here.'

What a cheek! What was *he* doing in the chapel? I don't suppose he was a vicar. He sounded too young.

When I didn't answer his question, he flashed a light right at me. Ow! It was blinding. I couldn't see a thing. I held my hand over my eyes and the Voice asked, 'Is anyone with you?'

'My sister,' I said. 'Didn't you hear her yelling? And if you don't switch that torch off, I'll let the dog go and she'll take your leg off.'

'OK. OK.' The light went out but it was a few minutes before my sight got back to normal.

'Come outside so we can talk,' I snapped. 'We're not thugs or anything.'

I headed towards the door and I heard him

scramble to his feet. I didn't turn round. I just walked out and waited for him to follow me. Kirstie was standing clinging to Dobbin, looking white-faced and scared.

'What's going on, Ally? Who's in there? Should we go?'

I was still hanging onto Lizzie's collar. 'No, we stay. Whoever he is, he's really frightened of something. Don't know what he's doing in there. Hiding probably.'

At that moment, he emerged from the chapel, stopping in the doorway as if he was terrified to come near us.

'You've got to tell me who you are and what you're doing here,' he said. He was American. Maybe fourteen or fifteen. Wearing cool jeans and a jacket – dirty but still cool.

'Why should we tell you?' I said.

But Kirstie butted in.

'We'll tell you, if you'll tell us why you were in the chapel.'

He nodded. 'OK. It's a deal. So you first. Why are you up here, miles from anywhere?'

I told him straight. 'Our dad went over to the mainland to fetch our grandad. The ferry must have been damaged in the storm and he's not come back yet.'

'So why aren't you waiting for him at home?'

'We haven't got a home,' said Kirstie. 'After that storm last night, there's nothing left except a ruin. We slept on a mattress on the floor.'

'OK, but you must have people you could go to.'

'You don't understand,' I said. 'Everyone's disappeared. The village looks like a warzone, everything's gone. The only people we've seen are a bunch of scary men with guns. Nobody's come over from the mainland to help, as though they don't know what's happened here.'

He didn't look surprised. It was as if he expected it.

'We're heading for Tarbay,' said Kirstie. 'It's the only other place on Shairn. It's on the far side of the island. There's sure to be somebody there.'

The boy frowned. 'Oh yes, there'll be people all right. But you mustn't go.'

'Why not?'

'Because that's the place I'm running away from.'

Chapter Thirteen

The temperature began to drop and the wind was growing stronger. Before the boy told us his story, we decided to go inside the chapel – the three of us, Lizzie and the horse.

'I just hope Dobbin doesn't do anything disgusting, that's all,' Kirstie said. 'The smell will be unbearable. I'd be sick.'

That's typical of my sister. It wasn't as if we had a choice of five-star hotels to stay in. We had been lucky to come across the chapel. We'd better make the most of it, that's what I thought. I helped her down from Dobbin and sat her over in the corner.

The boy told us that his name was Brad Holden. He'd been in Scotland for two months while his parents did some kind of research. They were marine biologists, he said – but I wasn't really sure what a marine biologist was except that they sounded dead brainy. I thought our dad was brainy because he worked with computers but somehow, a marine biologist sounded even brainier.

'Mom and Dad work at a university in California,' Brad told us. 'They study the sea and things that live in it. Mom's brother, Uncle Tom, is a scientist, too. He's been coming over here for several years. Doing research and stuff. He was interested in global warming and rising sea levels – really passionate about it. Two years ago he wrote a fantastic book about the changes in the weather.'

'Cor,' I said. 'Will we meet him? Is he over here now?'

'No. Last summer he found something here that worried him.'

'Like what?'

'I don't know exactly but he was emailing his findings to Mom and Dad.'

'Is that why they came over?' Kirstie asked. 'To take a look at what he'd found?'

He shuffled around a bit as if he was embarrassed. 'Not exactly. Well, partly...'

'Well, what?' I was feeling irritated. I can't stand people who don't come out with it. Anyway, I was hungry. I couldn't be bothered waiting for him to tell us his stupid story.

'Let's have something to eat. I'm starving,' I said and pulled the sandwiches and the cans of Coke out of my pockets. The cheese must have fallen out on the way.

'Coke?' said Kirstie. 'Yuk! Couldn't you even get a bottle of water?'

'Coke's my favourite,' I protested.

'It's full of horrible chemicals. Thanks to you, we're either going to die of starvation or chemical poisoning.'

My sister always exaggerates.

'I've got water,' said Brad, 'and I've got food. I brought plenty. We can share it.'

He stood up, switched on his torch and walked across to the far corner of the chapel. He bent down and felt around inside a bag. When he came back, he was carrying apples, oatcakes and a pack of cheese.

'Thanks, Brad. You're brilliant,' said Kirstie in her girlie voice and then she turned to give me one of her looks and stuck out her tongue. I should care!

'Go on then,' I said when I'd finished the sandwich. 'What was in your uncle's emails?'

'Scientific findings. It seemed that he had uncovered something that was very worrying. It was something serious – but I don't know what.'

'Then what happened?'

'Uncle Tom sent his findings every day for three weeks but they suddenly stopped.'

'Did he explain it all when he came back?'

'That's the whole point. He didn't come back.'

'You mean he disappeared?'

'Exactly. The university tried everything to find him. So did Mom and Dad. But they always drew a blank. This was where Uncle Tom was working when he disappeared. He was particularly interested in the whirlpools near here. They're not unique but they are unusual.'

I knew about them. Grandad had told me. In some places just off the coast, the sea swirled around like water going down a plughole. Since I was really small, Grandad had told us stories about fishermen being sucked down to the sea bed and coming back as ghosts to haunt the shores hereabouts.

'So your parents came over here to look for your uncle?'

He shook his head. 'No. They think he's dead.'

'Drowned?'

'More likely killed for what he found out.'

I gasped. 'You mean, he was murdered?' I said. 'So where have your parents gone?'

'To Tarbay to get proof about experiments that are affecting the atmosphere . . .'

'Atmosphere? You mean the air?'

'Sort of.'

'Could that have caused the storm that flattened Grandad's cottage?'

'Sure. Whatever they're doing is affecting the weather in a big way. Dad found a laboratory yesterday and he didn't like what he saw there.'

'What about the locals living in Tarbay?'

'According to Dad, there's nobody that looks like a Scottish fisherman. They all looked like the military.'

'Wearing black uniforms?'

'So he said.'

'And your dad went back again this morning?'

'Yeah. Mom's gone with him this time and they've taken cameras and recording equipment. They plan to send their findings to Edinburgh University then, depending on what they uncover, they'll contact the government.' Brad looked anxiously at the fading light. 'I'm worried. They should have been back by now. I hope they're OK.'

Daylight had almost gone. Brad reached for his torch and switched it on. I noticed for the first time it was a crazy sort of torch with a handle.

'Christmas present,' he said. 'Look, I crank the handle to power the torch. No more batteries, see?

You can always rely on something simple like this.'

Amazing! I decided to ask for one for my next birthday. I'd add it to my list.

When the daylight had finally gone, we decided we should go to sleep.

'I've got a blanket,' said Brad.

'We've got one, too.'

'Then we'll be warm enough.' He grinned at me. 'I can't tell you how scared I was when you guys arrived. Sorry I was so rude.'

'I bet you thought we were the Men in Black who'd tracked you down, eh?'

'Something like that.'

We tied Dobbin to one of the pillars near the door. We didn't want him stepping on us in the middle of the night. We lay on the floor and pulled Brad's blanket over us all. Lizzie, who was now walking brilliantly on three legs, came and snuggled next to me for extra warmth and I hugged her like a woolly hot-water bottle.

'So, why did your parents leave you here?' I asked Brad.

'Mom and Dad said it was too dangerous for me to go with them. I wanted to stay in the cave where we spent last night, but our boat is moored nearby.'

'Was that your boat we saw? Wow! It's a beauty.'

'Yes, but very visible. It might draw somebody's attention. If those men can kill my uncle...' Brad sounded really anxious. 'Let's hope Mom and Dad come back tomorrow. We have to get off this island – fast.'

Chapter Fourteen

The ground was hard but we didn't care. It was good to be out of the wind. We settled down and closed our eyes but, for some reason, Lizzie was twitchy and wouldn't stay still. Even though I had my arms round her, she moved about looking this way and that, finally wriggling out of my grasp. She was giving out small excited whines and we could hear her claws on the stone floor as she raced from one spot to the other.

'For goodness sake, Lizzie, come back and settle down.'

But it made no difference. She wouldn't come. As well as Lizzie's noises, there were squeaks like fingernails on a chalk board. Then scrabbling – first in one spot at the far end of the chapel and then nearer, close to our corner. They were small scratchy noises that made my skin creep.

It was Kirstie who spoke first.

'Brad. Where's the food?'

'I'm not sure. I guess I must have left it over by the door where we ate. I left it in my rucksack.'

I pretended to be asleep but I could feel Kirstie

shaking. She knew there were rats around. A place like this was probably full of them, nesting under the walls and in the holes where stones had broken away. Nice warm places for dozens and dozens of rats – feeding on the sacks of cattle food left by a kind farmer with a little extra food from us.

When something ran over the blanket, Kirstie screamed and sat bolt upright.

'Turn on the torch, Brad. There's something here. PLEASE TURN IT ON! PLEASE!'

The beam of the torch lit up the small area where we were lying and things looked almost normal until Brad flashed the light further away and we saw Lizzie racing on her three legs across the floor, chasing rats. The rats were fast but Lizzie was hungry and her empty belly made her faster. As a group of the rats disappeared into their hole, Lizzie caught the last and largest rat and sunk her teeth into it. She shook it violently from side to side until, with a final freakish squeak, the rat was dead. Lizzie walked towards us with the body of the dead rat hanging limp from her mouth, and flopped down on our blanket and began to tear it apart. She hadn't eaten since yesterday. It wasn't her fault if we couldn't stand the sight of blood and rat's entrails. She glanced up, still crunching the bones, as we yelled and leapt away from her.

'I need to get out of here,' said Kirstie, hopping towards the door. 'I can't stand it!' She flung it open and collapsed onto the hillside. We soon followed her. Brad brought the blankets and we crouched, shivering in the black, black night when the most amazing thing happened.

There was a crack of thunder and the sky was suddenly lit up with fork lightning. Shafts of lightning as far as the eye could see, filling the night sky. It was like watching the best firework display you've ever seen – and then some. We stood there transfixed by the sight of it.

Rain began to fall and the bitter wind whipped up even stronger than before.

There was more thunder followed by lightning.

'We should go back to the rats,' said Kirstie. 'At least we'd be dry.'

But Brad stood where he was, watching the sky. Trying to make sense of the lightning.

'You know what?' he said. 'It's moving fast. Every time it strikes it moves further along the coast. My bet is that it's heading for the same place the storm hit last night. That's odd.'

He was right. The lightning flashes finally hit the far side of the island. And there they stayed. It reminded me of those war films on telly where they're dropping bombs. It was just like that. Flash! Crash! Boom! But now all the bombs were falling on Caitlin, probably on our cottage. Again.

Kirstie was really upset. 'I don't like it. Please let's go back inside. It's horrible to think what's happening over there.'

We helped her back into the chapel, glad to be out of the cold and rain. We huddled in the corner. Brad put the torch on to keep the rats away.

'All this is really weird,' I said. 'Will your parents find out what's happening, Brad?'

'They're trying to.'

'But why are we the only ones that think anything is wrong? All these terrible storms. We might as well be on another planet. Nobody is coming to help. Why isn't anyone on the mainland wondering what's going on? Aren't they worried that people are getting killed over here?'

'Maybe they don't know,' said Kirstie.

'That's practically impossible,' said Brad. 'What about your dad? Don't you think he'll be going crazy because he can't get back to the island? Won't he have gone to the police to tell them you're alone over here? It doesn't make sense.'

'He'll think that Mrs Cameron will be looking after us, I suppose.'

Brad wasn't convinced.

We lay there but we found it difficult to sleep.

'What's going to happen tomorrow?' Kirstie asked.

'Mom and Dad will be back. You'll see. Don't worry. Everything will be OK.'

Where had I heard that before?

Chapter Fifteen

Seeing Lizzie hunt for food made us think seriously about survival. Lizzie could fend for herself and there was plenty of grass for Dobbin – but what about us? The next morning we discussed what food we had left. It was no more than a snack. I would fade away to nothing. My legs would be reduced to sticks. I would be able to play tunes on my ribs and a strong wind would probably blow me away.

'I usually have breakfast,' I said. 'Can't I have a biscuit or something? I'm starving.'

My sister told me to shut up as if my opinions didn't count.

'You're hopeless,' said Kirstie. 'We've nothing to drink. Even your stupid Coke cans are empty, Ally.'

'Water's not a problem,' Brad said, butting into our argument. 'This chapel was built on top of a spring. Come inside and I'll show you.'

Just to the right of the door was a block of stone and out of a hole in the centre bubbled clear, fresh water which fell into a stone trough and drained back into the ground.

'Mom said the chapel was put here for travellers

who got lost or needed shelter while they were crossing the island. She read about it. That's why I came here to hide. It was the perfect place.'

The sun was shining like it hadn't done for weeks so Brad and I decided to ride Dobbin to see if there were any signs of his mum and dad. At least it would take my mind off my empty stomach.

'Will you be OK by yourself?' Brad asked Kirstie.

'Of course. I'll just chill out. Get a tan – you know. I'll be fine. My ankle needs a rest.'

Dobbin seemed keen to go – glad to be outside and free to run. We rode back up the hill to the point I had reached yesterday. The point where we could see right across to Tarbay, the coastline and the sea.

'Stop over there on the other side of that rock,' said Brad. 'We don't want to be seen, do we?'

We climbed off Dobbin and lay down in the heather, leaning up on our elbows.

'Any sign of your mum and dad?'

He shook his head.

'We could wait here for a while. They'll probably come.'

We kept our gaze fixed on the path that led towards Tarbay. At first, we talked. I had plenty of questions.

'Tell me about your uncle and all this stuff about the weather.'

'What he found out last summer was to do with climate change. The stuff Dad saw yesterday in the lab was connected with that, too. My parents are very calm people, but it really bothered them. So they've gone to find evidence.'

'Evidence of what?'

'Evidence that someone was seriously messing with the weather.'

'Or controlling it, Brad. Just imagine, if you had control over the weather, you could control the world. A Mastermind.'

'That might sound like comic book stuff but maybe you're not so far from the truth. Dad got into the lab but he couldn't stay long. There were people about.'

'Wow! It's like James Bond.'

'Not really. The security wasn't great because who's to break in? There's no one left in Tarbay. And now your village has been destroyed.'

'No need to worry if you've bumped everybody off, eh?'

I felt horrified to think of all the people I knew on the island. Probably dead now.

We fell silent and just sat, watching. I could tell Brad was really worried that his parents hadn't come. He must have been thinking they'd been caught or something. I was feeling nervous, too – wondering when we'd ever see Dad again – and I suppose we'd almost given up hope when we suddenly saw the whoosh of a flare coming up from the sea to the north of the island. It was like the best rocket you get on bonfire night and it shot miles high into the sky and seemed to keep on going.

Brad leapt to his feet like a cork out of a bottle. 'It's them! That's where the boat is. They're sending a signal.'

'Are you sure? It might be the men from the laboratory.'

'Wait. If they send another flare in a few seconds, I'll be sure.'

I wanted to know why his parents hadn't come to the chapel like they said. But Brad was too busy focusing his eyes on one spot. I would have to wait for the answer.

When the second flare shot into the sky, Brad acted like he had springs on his feet, whooping for joy and bouncing over the heather.

'Come on, Ally. Let's get moving,' he said, untying

Dobbin from a tree stump. 'We've got to get to the cave.'

We both climbed on Dobbin and rode at full pelt to the chapel to collect Kirstie and Lizzie.

'Leave everything,' said Brad. 'Just get on the horse, Kirstie, and hold onto Lizzie. There's no time to waste. I'll explain as we go along.'

Brad ran ahead while I led Dobbin and for a time we went along the path the way we had come yesterday then, under instruction from Brad, we veered off the path and headed for the cliff edge. Kirstie began to look nervous.

'Where are we going, Brad? This is getting dangerously close to the edge. The ground could break away or something.'

But Brad assured us that he knew what he was doing. 'See over there?' he said, pointing a few metres away. 'There are steps cut into the rock. We can walk down to the beach. That's how we'll get to the cave.'

'ARE YOU MAD?' Kirstie shouted. 'How can I walk down there with this ankle?'

Brad patted the horse's neck.

'Dobbin can walk down, Kirstie. He'll carry you. No worries. Just wrap your arms round his neck and hang on. I'll lead him. Ally can carry Lizzie. Is that OK?'

I thought my sister was going to be sick – but as far as I could see, we just had to do it. The steps would eventually take us to where Brad's parents and their boat were waiting.

Next step – the mainland.

Chapter Sixteen

My sister made a bit of a fuss but, really, the steps were quite wide and not too steep. There was a metal handrail fixed into the cliff wall, so we held onto that.

'Please go slowly,' Kirstie said. 'I daren't even open my eyes. I just know it's a terrible drop to the beach. Don't let go of the rope, will you, Brad?'

Dobbin did really well. Brad talked to him as he led him and we took it steady. Kirstie looked like a sack of potatoes clinging onto him.

'Nearly there,' Brad said. 'Another six or seven steps, that's all.'

Once we were on the shingle, I couldn't resist tearing off my trainers and running into the sea where I stood feeling the ice cold waves lap against my legs and soothing my blisters.

'Come in,' I yelled. 'The water's great!'

Brad helped Kirstie down and led Dobbin to cool off in the shallows. Lizzie was already with me. It was fantastic to be in the water, laughing and shouting and feeling normal.

But Brad didn't stay with us. He was soon off,

racing down the beach. And when a woman appeared waving frantically and running towards him, he shouted, 'Mom!' over and over again until he reached her. Then she flung her arms round him and they hugged like they hadn't met for years. They must have been worried to death about each other. Abandoning her son in a strange place couldn't have been easy.

Brad looked back, beckoning us to come and join them. So we headed down the beach. Kirstie insisted on hopping with one arm round my shoulder.

'Mom, this is Alexandra and Kirstie. They dropped into the chapel to see me,' he said and turned to us, grinning. 'Guys, I'd like you to meet my mom.'

The first things I noticed were her boots – strong walking boots which were well worn. And her hair was an amazing colour, like gold and silver mixed, and tied in a thick plait that fell down her back. She had a smile like Brad's and looked really friendly. He was lucky to have a mum like that. She reminded me of mine and I felt sad. I missed her.

She held out her hand. 'I'm so pleased to meet you both,' she said. 'Please call me Kim. You guys must have a lot to tell me. Come on. Let's go to the cave.'

We walked along the beach and past the boat which was anchored a few metres out.

'Are we leaving soon?' Brad asked. 'Ally and Kirstie have seen some of those guys you saw at the laboratory.'

'Leaving in broad daylight would be too dangerous, Brad. We might be seen. We're leaving after dark.'

'Where's Dad?'

She shook her head. 'There's a lot to tell you, sweetheart, but not now.'

Brad shrugged. 'I don't understand.'

Kim frowned a little and put her hands on Brad's shoulder.

'Dad's been hurt,' she said.

'Badly?'

'Let's go see him. He's in the cave.' Then she noticed Kirstie trying to hobble along. 'Here,' she said. 'Let me give you a hand, Kirstie. That leg looks bad.'

'I think it's broken.'

'Or maybe a really bad sprain. I've got something that will help. And I'll find you something to eat. There might even be an apple for your horse, too.' She smiled as she wrapped her arm round Kirstie to support her. 'Come on, guys. Let's go see Dad.'

The entrance to the cave was hidden by boulders and rocky outcrops. From a distance it was not visible but when we got closer, I could see that the entrance was like a huge split in the rock face. Brad's mum led us inside – all of us, even Dobbin. The entrance was barely a metre wide – but was as high as a cathedral door. To help us down the dark passageway, we put our hands on the walls and shuffled over the gritty floor, one behind the other. Occasionally we would trip and bump into each other but as we turned the last corner, the passage opened out into a round cave like the room of a house. It was lit by candles and smelled of the sea. From a corner of the ceiling, there was water dripping continuously. Drip, drip, drip. We were under the hill, it was cold and I couldn't help but shiver.

Brad pushed his way past me and went over to the far side where someone was lying on the ground, covered in a sleeping bag, his eyes closed.

'Dad! Are you all right?' Brad said as he knelt by his side and held his hand. The man's eyes flickered open, he smiled and reached out his hand.

'Glad you're back, son,' he said. 'Sorry we didn't make it to the chapel. Slight problem.'

But Kim gently pulled Brad away.

'Let him rest, sweetheart. Come over here and I'll explain.'

They moved away before she began.

'We got into the laboratory all right – at least Dad did. Their security isn't great. I stayed outside to keep a lookout. He'd been in there for ten minutes or so when I saw one of the men coming. I tapped on the door to warn him and we ran out of the compound. We'd intended to head straight back to you in the chapel but there were more of them on the hillside.'

'You mean those men in military uniform?' I asked. 'Black? Really scary?'

'You've seen 'em, huh? Well, the only way to avoid them was along the shore.'

'So what happened to Dad? Did he have an accident?'

She stared at her feet. 'No. One of them saw him. I was well ahead so I don't think he saw me but he shouted something vile at Dad and reached for his gun. It was awful. Awful!' Obviously still upset by what had happened, she broke down in tears and Brad put his arms round her to comfort her. 'I felt so helpless,' she sobbed into his chest. 'There was nothing I could do.'

She cried for a while and then Brad asked, 'So what then?'

She looked at him, wiping away a tear. 'That man fired two shots. The first one struck Dad's shoulder. The second hit the middle of his back and he fell to the ground. Of course the man thought he had killed him.'

'How come he hadn't? It sounds like a pretty clear shot.'

Brad's mum smiled weakly. 'Dad was carrying his camera case with the strap across his body – buckles and all. The bullet struck a piece of metal and that saved Dad's life. The impact knocked him over and he stayed lying on the ground absolutely still. The man was walking over to check that he was dead when a siren sounded at the base and he ran off.'

Brad glanced across at his dad. 'How did you get him back here, Mom?'

'He was losing a lot of blood from the shoulder wound. I strapped it up as best I could and he managed to walk leaning against me – but it took a long time.'

'Is he going to be OK?'

'The medicines I had on the boat will help. But he's weak, Brad. We've got six or seven hours before the light goes. If he's a little stronger by then, we'll get him onto the boat. We need to leave soon. It's only a matter of time before they spot the boat.'

Brad shut his eyes to blot out the horror of what had happened. When he opened them again he said, 'And the evidence, Mom? What did Dad find?'

She shook her head. 'There was nothing. He tried taking photos but, for some reason, his camera didn't work. After all the risks we took, we didn't get a thing.'

I could see from the expression on Brad's face that he was shocked. 'So you mean we've gone through all this and we've still got no proof of what's going on?'

'All we can do now is tell the authorities about the storms and what we've seen at the lab.'

Brad lost his rag. 'And why should they believe you, Mom?' he said, pacing backwards and forwards. 'A few bad storms around an island – so what? They'll put it down to global warming. They'll dismiss you as some kind of crazy woman with an overactive imagination. You know they won't act on anything you say without proof.'

No one said anything. We stood in silence with only the drip, drip, drip of the water.

But Brad's fury was still bubbling up. He was bursting with anger. 'We can't just leave, Mom! We have to get some *proof* of what's going on. It's what Uncle Tom would want and you know it's what Dad would want, too. He wouldn't give up. It's too important. No. WE CAN'T GIVE UP!'

Kim sank down on a rocky ledge. 'And I can't go back. It's too risky. What would happen to you and Dad if I got caught?' She sat up straight, knowing that she had made the decision. 'No. I won't do it, Brad. That's final. When night falls, we sail for the mainland.'

Chapter Seventeen

Brad stormed out of the cave without a word.

His mum looked grey with worry. 'Go after him, will you, Ally? He's very upset. He thinks I've let him down. Go talk to him. Please.'

I ran down the beach and caught up with him. We walked along side by side for some time without speaking. Then he said, 'How could she do this? How can she leave the island without getting proof of what's happening here? She said that Dad had broken into the lab easily. So what's the problem? Why not try again? I could go with her. I could help.'

I waited until he'd calmed down.

'What makes you think you could do any better than your dad?'

'I could look for papers – records of experiments they've been doing – and we could take them and show them to people who matter. The papers should be proof enough of what's going on.'

I wasn't impressed by his plan. 'Who keeps records on paper nowadays?' I said as we walked on down the beach. 'The only thing to do would be to hack into their computers. That's where their data will be stored.'

'Silly me!' he said in a sarcastic tone. 'Why didn't I think of that? Hack into the computers – how simple is that?'

'It's not difficult when you know how. Honest.'

He stopped and turned to look at me. 'You mean you know how to do it?'

I nodded.

'You're kidding! You know about computers? Seriously?'

'Didn't you know I'm a computer genius? I take after my dad. He works with them day in, day out. He's taught me loads.'

He stood directly in front of me gripping my shoulders tight.

'Then you could help. We could get proof. We could do it together.'

'Oh no,' I protested, backing away. 'Your mum said not to. We're getting out of here tonight.'

I felt his eyes boring into me. I've never seen anyone so determined.

'I won't leave this place without finding what we came for. We have to prove what experiments are being carried out here. If these people can control this island, where will they stop? They'll move on to bigger things, that's for sure. We have to stop them, Ally. Time is running out.'

'No, I...'

'If we go now, we could be back before dark.'

'Impossible.'

'We can go the direct route. We can do it, Ally! WE CAN DO IT!'

This was all happening too fast. I felt that panicky feeling in my stomach, not certain what I should do. Should I go back and tell Kim what we were planning? Should I say, 'No way!'? Or should I grab the moment and help Brad? My mind was whirring.

'You've got to tell your mum what you're doing.'

'No. She'll try to stop me. I'm going now whether you come with me or not. Well? What's your answer?'

I turned to look at him and said, 'OK. I'm up for it.'

He slapped me on the arm. 'Good man! Good man! Let's go.'

I had to stop him in his tracks. He was too eager to leave.

'We'll need a disc to copy the data. We can't do anything without one.'

'No problem. There are some in the locker. We record soundings from the ocean bed, so we use them all the time. Come on. We'll get them.'

We ran down the beach and waded out to the boat. Brad climbed up a small metal ladder onto the deck, disappeared into the cabin, and came out with a box of discs.

'Just one,' I said, pulling it out. 'Or maybe two... Yes, two.'

Then we set off up the cliff steps and cut across the moor, planning to make a beeline for the lab. After a while, we saw the chapel in the distance to our right as we headed west and then it was another hour before we saw the coast.

The hillside, which fell steeply away, was thick with heather and bracken and they provided excellent cover for us.

As we came closer to Tarbay, we saw a long low building on the outskirts of the village which I assumed was the laboratory. It was made of units – a bit like those temporary offices on a building site, coated in what looked like white plastic. There were five of them linked together. I could only see two small windows along the side of the block and so finding a way in could be difficult. But worse still was the heavy metal fence that surrounded the lab. It was two metres high or more. There might even be razor wire at the top. How were we going to get over that? It would be impossible. I tried not to feel too depressed. After all, Brad's dad had managed to find a way in. So would we.

I squatted on my heels, peering through the bracken. 'Now we're so close, we've got to keep low and out of sight,' I said. 'I know your dad told you their security was poor, but if they see us, they'll shoot. Just like they shot poor Lizzie.'

Brad nodded. 'Probably Uncle Tom, too. You're right. We stay on guard. We only have one chance – and this is it.'

Chapter Eighteen

We flopped full-length onto the ground and then, commando-style, we pulled ourselves forward on our elbows. Through the heather and bracken. Down the hillside. Until we were fifty metres or so from the perimeter fence. Then, quite suddenly, a terrifying noise erupted from somewhere inside the compound. It was such an unearthly screeching and screaming that we froze, not daring to move a muscle, burying our heads in the undergrowth. We didn't know what was happening. We just had to wait, still as stone.

First there were footsteps – heavy footsteps – and then we heard a man's voice, coarse and very loud.

'SHUT IT, WILL YER?' he yelled. The screeching faded a little, but not much, and we gingerly parted the bracken in front of our faces and looked to see what was going on. A powerful man, dressed in the same black uniform I had seen the day before, marched into the compound. He bent down and flung something into a large cage on the far side.

I looked across at Brad. He shrugged his shoulders as if to say that he didn't know what was going on.

The terrible noise fell silent but we waited until the man walked away around the other side of the building.

'Time to move,' whispered Brad.

Keeping as low to the ground as we could, we wriggled forward down the hill towards the fence but, as we reached the wire, the screeching started once again. Whatever was in that cage had heard us. They were better than guard dogs. We crouched in the bracken by the fence and waited, almost deafened by the terrible noise. Once again the man came running into the compound shouting. This time he had a gun in his hand.

'SHUT IT, I SAID!' And he fired into the air.

Through the stalks we could now see what was making the noise and what was making the soldier so angry. In a huge, mesh cage were four fearsome birds violently flapping their enormous black wings. Their heads and necks were devoid of feathers and their beaks were hooked and vicious. I knew what they were.

'Vultures,' I hissed.

Brad shook his head. 'They can't be. Vultures don't make much noise.'

'Well, they *look* like vultures.'

'I didn't know you had them in Scotland.'

'We don't. There's something weird about these.'

The man fired the gun once again but nothing would silence the birds. The noise was indescribable. More men in black uniforms came running round the corner.

'Idiot!' one of them shouted. 'That won't do any good.'

'Well, I'm pissed off with 'em,' said the one with the gun. 'They sound off day and night. I'm fed up with their racket. Whose idea was it to have 'em 'ere?'

'No business of yours, soldier!' called a voice as a man appeared from the far side of the laboratory. He was taller than any of the others. His jaw was square and his eyes were black and mean. In fact, everything about him looked brutal – even his thick red hair was cut short like a yard brush. I decided to call him Brush Head.

'These birds are a part of our experiments, aren't they, soldier?' he mocked. 'And we're here to carry out experiments, aren't we. That's what we're paid for – not to play around firing guns in the air. IS THAT CLEAR?'

'Yes, sir,' said the soldier, who was standing to

attention, staring straight ahead and shaking in his boots.

'Then give 'em some food to shut 'em up.'

'I have, sir.'

'BUT NOT ENOUGH, MAN!' Brush Head barked.

'Right, sir.'

The soldier hurried over to the cage, picked up a large plastic bucket and tipped the contents through the mesh. The birds pounced, squawking and quarrelling, until each had grabbed its own piece of dead flesh and began to tear at it with its fearsome, hooked beak.

'Now, down to the jetty, all of you,' he snapped. 'There's a boat coming in. Provisions, probably.'

There was a muttering amongst the men as if they were reluctant to go.

'AT THE DOUBLE!' Brush Head yelled and they immediately turned and jogged towards the gate, unlocked it and went through like a flock of black crows.

They were tall, hefty and well built. Strong like rugby players. All except a round, flabby one who I recognised at once.

Brad looked across at me. 'The Men in Black, eh?' he said as the soldiers headed away.

I nodded and grinned. 'I've seen the one with the bald head and the wobbly bum before,' I said. 'I called him the Sumo Wrestler.'

Brad burst out laughing but he managed to clap his hand over his mouth to stop the noise.

'Mom said they're all living in the old cottages. So they must have got rid of anyone who lived in the village.'

'Just like Caitlin,' I said. 'There was no one left there either.'

Eventually, when we were sure the men were well on their way to Tarbay, we got to our feet. 'Let's go check it out while we've got the chance,' said Brad. 'They didn't lock the gate – bad security.'

Running in a low crouch, we crossed the compound. Then we looked around the building, searching for a way in. We saw three small windows – all shut – and, on the far side, there was a door with a steel box set on the wall next to it. Over the box was a screen with a grille underneath.

'What's that?'

Brad shook his head. 'I'm not sure but it could be a hand-print recognition unit. You place your hand flat on the screen and it opens the lock. It'll be programmed only to let in certain people.'

'Cool! Let's try it.'

I was about to put my hand up but Brad grabbed me and pulled me away.

'Are you crazy? Do you want to set the alarm off?'

It probably wasn't a good idea.

'I thought you said the security was rubbish here.'

'It is. But that doesn't mean you go blundering in like a wild elephant. Take it easy, Ally. We'll find a way in.'

There was no handle so I pushed the door just to check. It didn't budge. It looked as if it locked automatically.

'How did your mum and dad get in? Did they tell you?'

'One of the doors was unlocked.'

'Wow! That was a piece of luck, eh? Well, they've definitely locked this one.'

We worked our way round and found another door at the far end of the last unit. That was locked too but it had a different security device which was a small box with buttons on it, each with a number.

'We'd need the number code to get in,' Brad explained – not that he needed to. There was one just like it at school.

'We could try tapping them at random.'

Brad wasn't keen. 'Let's leave that as a last resort. It's not likely to work and it's probably connected to an alarm system. Let's go check the windows again. If they're all shut we'll come back and try the code.'

I didn't think there was any chance. How stupid would that be to leave a window open? But I was wrong. One window with frosted glass had an opening at the top. At first glance, it looked shut but in fact the catch hadn't been fastened properly. Brad, who was quite a bit taller than me, reached up and pulled at the window. But it wouldn't move.

'I could do it if I had something to force it with,' he said. 'It hasn't been locked.'

I had just the thing. Grandad had given me a small Swiss army knife last summer. It's an amazing knife with lots of bits and pieces. I find it really useful when I'm looking for fossils.

I pulled it out of my pocket and handed it to Brad.

'Brilliant. You're a star, Ally. That's just what I need.'

With the knife in his hand, he reached up and pushed the blade into the tiny gap below the opening section of the window. In seconds he had prised it open.

'Fantastic!' I said. 'What now?'

Brad stood there, his hands on his hips, looking up at the opened window which was almost half a metre above his head. It was then that I got a nasty, uncomfortable feeling at the back of my neck.

'I guess this is where you do your bit,' he said.

'How do you mean?'

'If you climb on my shoulders, I guess you're small enough to get through that opening. Then you could open that back door. It shouldn't be a problem from the inside.'

How could I say no?

It was quite scary on Brad's shoulder – it was so high up – but it was even worse when I pushed my head through the window and looked down on the other side.

'This is the loo,' I called back. 'And somebody's left the seat up. What if I fall in headfirst?'

'You won't,' he said – but that was easy for him to say. He wasn't the one who was going to have his head jammed in the toilet.

Brad told me he would hold onto my ankles and lower me down slowly. He wouldn't let me drop. Honest. Well, this worked fine, but it only took me as far as the lavatory cistern. So there I was – dangling like a worm on a hook. I put my hands flat on the cistern, which seemed safe enough, then Brad let go of my ankles and I had to wriggle through the window in a sort of somersault, doing my best to avoid falling into the pan.

I landed on the floor with a thump and banged my head on the loo. I was glad that no one was around to hear me yell.

'You OK?'

'Yep,' I called back, rubbing the bump that was swelling on the back of my head. 'Just give me a minute and I'll find the door.'

The lavatory door opened into a changing room full of lockers. There were hooks on the wall and, hanging from them, were ten or twelve white protective suits. There were helmets and everything – but I didn't have time to look. I hurried past and out into a corridor which was lit by strip lights. There were doors on either side – all of them had labels set in small metal frames.

Right at the end of the corridor, I finally found the door I was looking for. A notice read EMERGENCY EXIT. It had no wires or buttons. No bolts, even. There was just one lock and that looked no more serious than the one we had at home. I turned it, pulled back the door and let Brad in.

Chapter Nineteen

We walked down the long corridor looking at the labels on the doors. They had letters and numbers on them which we couldn't understand – with the exception of one door which had a name on it – Dr X Frankwall.

'Who has a name beginning with X?' I said.

'Xavier is a French name. And then there's Xerxes, the King of Persia.'

'Sounds spooky to me.'

Brad tried the handle on the door but it was locked. Some of the others were locked, too but we found one that wasn't and we went in.

It was a square room with a square table in the middle on which was a map of the island with Tarbay and Caitlin clearly marked.

'Why are there pins stuck in it?'

Brad stopped and looked and shook his head. Coloured round-headed pins had been stuck in the map and a line of cotton ran from each pin to a label. We were particularly interested in a group of pins round Grandad's cottage. This is what we read on the labels:

July 21st W R H 2/3 miles shortfall of Caitlin.
July 28th Th R Adjusted targeting 2 miles. 1 mile
shortfall. Farm/cottage zero.
July 29th Th L Adjusted targeting 1 mile. All
buildings.

'We can't wait to work it out,' Brad said. 'Come on.'

The next room we found was a huge science lab. I don't know what I was expecting but it was just like ours at school. Nothing hi-tech at all. There were benches and high stools. Sinks and sockets and locked cabinets – you know the kind of thing. The only odd thing was a glassed-off area at one end. We hadn't a clue what that was for. I found an incubator on the far wall and inside were several eggs. Not hen's eggs. These were much bigger.

'Maybe vultures' eggs,' I said. 'Could they be breeding a new strain?'

'We're not interested in zoo stuff. We need the data about the storms. Don't let's hang around,' said Brad, heading for the door. 'The men could be back so we need to find the computer – come on.'

I followed him out into the corridor. 'How long do you think we've got?'

'Possibly a half hour. And the problem is, this building is soundproof. Have you noticed how quiet it is? Can't hear the sea, even. We won't have any warning when they come back.'

Brad's estimate of half an hour was way out. Minutes later, there was a rattle at the front door, then a buzz as someone's handprint was identified and the lock was released. The Men in Black had returned already and we were standing in the corridor.

Without thinking, we fled back to the changing room. I intended to leave the building the same way I had come in – through the lavatory window. No big deal. But it suddenly struck me that Brad would be too big to do the same.

'How are you going to get out?' I asked, once we were in the changing room.

'I'm not. I'm going to stay,' he said. 'We're still in with a chance of getting the data. Go if you want to, Ally, but I'm staying.' Then he pointed up high. 'I'll hide on top of the lockers. If anyone comes in, they're not gonna look up.'

'If you're staying, I'm staying,' I said. 'Give me a leg up. There's room up there for me.'

I stood on one of the benches and Brad helped

me to pull myself onto the top of a row of lockers where I lay stretched out, making myself as flat as possible. Brad did the same on the other side of the room so that we were facing each other as we waited. But what were we waiting for? I hoped that the men would leave the building in a short while and go back to the village so that we would have time to get out through the side door. That's what I hoped.

Instead, we heard them walking down the corridor – a steady brisk march. Footsteps getting closer all the time. There was no doubt about it, they were heading for the changing room. We hardly dared to breathe as the door opened and a group of men – ten or twelve of them – burst in. Maybe they were the same group we had seen earlier. It was hard to tell, dressed in the same black uniforms. But the first one I recognised as Brush Head.

'I didn't expect him today,' he snapped in his gravelly, rasping tone. 'But then I just follow orders.'

'He was here yesterday,' said one of the soldiers. 'Why's he come again? There's a problem, ain't there?'

'Don't ask questions – MOVE!' Brush Head yelled. 'Protective gear on – at the double!'

The men went immediately to their lockers.

Nobody looked up and so nobody saw us. They just stripped off their black suits. Everything. Right down to their underpants. I had a brilliant view of the Sumo Wrestler – the flabbiest of the lot. He looked ridiculous without clothes. Not only did his bottom wobble but his belly drooped over his underpants which were blue with pink spots and hung loose down to his knees. This was the man who was so scary when he had a vicious dog on the end of the lead – but just look at him now!

'Thirty seconds!' Brush Head barked. 'I want you all in the control lab.'

The men had changed into white bodysuits with white rubber boots. All but Brush Head pulled helmets on. The dark visors covering their eyes reminded me of a page in my biology book with a picture of a fly's head. That's exactly what they looked like – a swarm of flies. Huge, nasty buzzing flies. What were they doing on Shairn? Why were they here?

We heard the door slam and suddenly the room was quiet again. The men were gone.

'You were right,' I hissed. 'They didn't see us.'

Brad was already climbing down off the lockers.

'What are you doing?' I said.

He pointed to the suits hanging on the hooks. 'These must be for visitors and I guess I'm a visitor. There should be one that fits.' He took one, held it up to check the size and then pulled it on over his jeans. 'I'm going to join them and find out what they're up to.'

I couldn't believe what I was hearing. 'Are you mad? You can't.'

'They'll never notice me in the crowd. I'm tall enough to look like them. Trust me.' He stepped into the suit. 'You stay there, Ally. I'll be back before you know it.'

He zipped up the front of the suit and pulled on the helmet so that he looked just like all the others. I shut my eyes as he walked away. I couldn't bear it. This was crazy. This was stupid. This was dangerous.

I lay on the locker feeling alone and totally helpless. All I could do was keep my fingers crossed and wait.

When the door suddenly opened a few minutes later, I thought he had returned. I peeped over the edge but quickly pulled back. It wasn't Brad. I wished it had been. It was none other than Dracula himself. He marched in followed by Brush Head,

121

who was carrying his helmet under his arm.

'My suit, Trudor,' Dracula barked at Brush Head. 'I need to get this business sorted out and I haven't much time.'

Brush Head was sifting through the suits on the pegs on the opposite side of the room. But it was obvious that he couldn't find the one he needed.

'Come on, man. What's the matter?'

'It doesn't seem to be here, Dr Frankwall. I can't understand ...'

Dracula looked irritated and pushed Brush Head aside. He took a suit which seemed near enough in size and pulled that on.

'This is typical of bad management. My name is stamped across the back, is it not? Find out who took it and report them to me. But not at the moment. We have urgent work to do.'

I was panic-stricken. It was obvious that Brad had taken the doctor's bodysuit and, without knowing it, the words DR X FRANKWALL were written across the back for all to see. He was in a room surrounded by the enemy and he was sure to be found out.

Chapter Twenty

Have you ever had to wait for something? You know – when you wait and wait and wait and nothing happens? That afternoon was like that. After Dracula had left, nothing happened for ages and I just lay on top of the lockers, crazy with worry. Early on, the muscle in my left leg started to tense up and I knew what was coming. Cramp! It spread slowly from the calf muscle down the leg and into my foot until my toes tensed up and I almost screamed with the pain of it. I managed to stop myself yelling by biting on one hand while rubbing my leg with the other and, eventually, it went away.

All this time, I tried not to think about Brad. I started counting the lockers, then the tiles on the floor and the screws in the doors. But when my bladder began to cry out to be emptied, I decided that it wasn't much of a risk to climb down off the locker and slip into the lavatory. Nobody would come, I thought. They were most likely having a meeting.

Getting down off the locker was easier than I thought and once my feet were on the ground, I went over to the door and pressed my ear to it and listened for any sounds. There was nothing. I was safe for the time being. It was great to be standing upright again and, after I'd been to the toilet, I did a few exercises – touching toes, twisting, that kind of thing – then I jumped onto the bench ready to climb up to my hiding place.

Of course, you've guessed it, I couldn't get back. I had forgotten that I needed Brad's help in the first place. How could I forget that? I reached up but it was impossible. No matter how I tried, the locker was too high for me to pull myself up. I couldn't even grip the edge. Now what?

I had no safe place to hide. If I stayed in the locker room I'd be seen as soon the men came back. My only hope was to get out through the same window and wait on the hillside until Brad came – *if* he came. I went into the lavatory and, as I stood on the seat, I heard a noise in the locker room. They were back already. I was getting out in the nick of time. I stepped up onto the cistern and put my hands on the open window, ready to pull myself up. But in my panic, my foot slipped. I couldn't stop myself – I fell backwards, knocking the lid off the cistern. So the lid and I fell together, crashing to the floor.

As I lay there crumpled in a heap in the small cubicle, the door opened. I screwed up my eyes and waited.

'What are you doing in there?'

It was Brad.

I looked up. 'It's a long story.'

He helped me to my feet and pushed the broken bits of the cistern lid into the corner.

'We've got to get out, Brad. They'll have heard all that noise for sure.'

'I don't think so. They're at the other end of the building.'

'So?'

'So if we move quickly, we'll get the data from the computer. I know where it is.'

'How?'

'Don't ask. Just follow me.'

We hurried out of the changing room and turned left down the corridor to the door with Dr X Frankwall written on it.

'Isn't it locked?'

It obviously wasn't, because Brad opened it and walked in.

'Got the disc?'

'Got it.'

A computer was on the desk and, displayed on

the screen, were the words STORM CONTROL project: small island. Underneath was a list of files, each one numbered and dated. This was a massive piece of luck. I didn't have to hack into the computer after all. Someone had turned it on and left the room. I wanted to ask a hundred questions – but there was no time. I had to copy the files stored in the computer and that could take several minutes. I looked towards the door. It was still shut.

'Don't let them come in,' I kept saying to myself as I slipped the disc into the slot. 'Don't let them come in.' And a cold sweat broke out on my forehead.

I tried to stay calm. I highlighted the list of files on the screen, clicked on SEND TO DISC and waited.

I was expecting a bar to be displayed on the screen, showing the progress of the copying, but instead there was a message.

YOUR DATA CANNOT BE SAVED
CORRUPT DISC

'It's damaged,' I said.

'Try the other one,' said Brad. 'You did bring two, didn't you?'

I nodded. My hands were shaking as I removed the

first disc, replaced it with the second one and waited.

Same result.

We realised that the discs could have been corrupted – maybe the storm had done it or the lightning or the sea water. There were too many possibilities. Now we had no means of copying the data.

'Over there,' Brad said, pointing to a shelf on the wall. 'We can use one of those.'

There was a pile of thin white boxes on which was written

FRANKWALL RESEARCH

CD – R120

PROTECTED RECORDABLE

I opened one of the plastic cases, took out the CD and slipped it into the computer. This time it worked and a bar appeared on the screen:

Saving data.

Estimated time left: 2 minutes 15 seconds

And the familiar whirring noise from the computer began.

We fixed our eyes on the screen and watched as the bar filled and the time ticked by. There was nothing we could do to speed things up.

1 minute 45 seconds.

1 minute 13 seconds.

55 seconds.

21 seconds.

Then we heard a noise. Someone was coming.

15 seconds.

They were getting nearer.

8 seconds.

3 seconds.

YOUR DOCUMENTS ARE NOW COPIED
PLEASE REMOVE YOUR DISC

Someone stopped outside the door as I pressed the eject button and removed the disc. Brad grabbed the plastic case and we both dived under the desk as the door opened and someone walked in. Would he see us? I closed my eyes and stopped breathing.

He pulled out the chair in front of the computer and sat down, missing me by a whisker. I pressed my back to the wall as hard as I could and Brad did the same. We both prayed that he wouldn't stretch his legs and catch us with his feet. As he tapped on the keyboard, we crouched in that tiny space.

'Trudor!' he shouted and I recognised the voice of Dracula – alias Dr Frankwall. He was sitting centimetres away from us and I tried hard not to shake – but it was impossible.

Within seconds, Brush Head had arrived to the doctor's call.

'I shall go back now and consider the findings,' Dracula said. 'Yesterday we reduced every building on the far side of the island to rubble.' He paused as if he was enjoying the thought of it. 'Good but not yet good enough. I need more than one little island. I need to destroy a city, Trudor! Edinburgh will do nicely, I think. *Then* I will have completed my work. I will have the proof of the power of Storm Control. Think of it! I have created a fearsome weapon using the weather itself.' He rocked in his chair as his evil spine-chilling laugh filled the room. Then he went silent for a moment. 'There is a list of wealthy men desperate to buy this weapon, Trudor, and I will not risk being found out at this stage. My network of spies tell me people are asking questions on the mainland. There could be a threat to Storm Control and so we must leave immediately.' He pushed his chair back and stood up. 'There are exciting times ahead. If all goes well, Edinburgh will be destroyed.'

Trudor muttered something in agreement and the doctor continued.

'Go now. Dismantle everything at once. All the equipment. This building. Everything. Take the birds, too. There must be no evidence that we have been here.'

'Of course, doctor. I shall see that it's done.'

We heard the click of a mouse and the dying whisper of the computer as he turned it off. Then Dracula walked out of the room, switching off the lights and slamming the door shut behind him. For a time, he spoke out in the corridor and then we heard the main door open and close.

'I think he just left,' I whispered. 'It's worse than I thought.'

Brad nodded.

We had what we came for but now it was vital than we got it to the mainland as fast as we could. The threat to Edinburgh was imminent. But for the next few minutes, we would have to wait until we were sure everyone had left the building.

It was not long before we heard footsteps down the corridor as the men went into the locker room to change out of the white suits (we guessed). We could hear them talking – probably relieved that Dracula had gone. Then suddenly we heard angry shouts and sounds of fighting and I wondered if one of them had spotted the broken lid in the toilet. Maybe one had blamed another – that's often how fights break out, particularly among stupid people and the Men in Black weren't the brightest candles on the cake.

Trudor, who must have been out in the corridor, bellowed, 'SHUT IT! GET DOWN TO THE SHEDS. BRING THE TRUCKS AND THE TOOLS. I WANT THIS PLACE REMOVED! FAST!'

The quarrel stopped. There was some muttering we couldn't hear and, shortly after, there was the noise of boots – those heavy black boots – going down to the main door. A door opened. Men walked out. A door slammed shut.

Now was the time to leave Dracula's office and get away.

We opened the door slowly and looked out. The corridor was clear. The easy way out would be through the side door – the one with the simple lock on it, that Brad had come through. We walked cautiously down the corridor, holding our breath until we could be sure that we were alone.

We were halfway down when a terrible thing happened. I couldn't believe it. The door of the changing room opened and I was suddenly face to face with the Sumo Wrestler – right there in the corridor. He was as shocked as I was but when he glanced over my shoulder and saw Brad still in his white suit, he must have thought there was an explanation for me being there. I was only a kid after all.

It was that split second of hesitation that gave us our chance.

Chapter Twenty-One

Head down, Brad ran at his stomach, striking it hard with his helmet. Sumo's jaw fell open in surprise and he dropped the black plastic bag he was carrying. From the clatter of broken pottery, we guessed that the bag contained the remains of the cistern lid.

But his stomach was not as wobbly as we had thought. It was all tough muscle and Brad bounced back against the wall. Sumo grabbed his collar with one hand and lifted him off his feet. He dragged his helmet off with the other hand, roaring as he did so, and flung it on the ground. Then he balled his hand into a fist and raised it, ready to smash into Brad's face.

I had to do something.

Everything happened so quickly. Sumo's back was towards me so I swung my leg as hard as I could and struck the back of his knee. WHAM! One leg buckled. WHAM! I did it again so that the other leg went from under him and he was unable to stop himself from plummeting to the floor. He was so heavy that he fell with a mighty crash, banging his head on the wall as he dropped.

'You OK?' I asked Brad.

'Yeah. What about him?'

Sumo wasn't moving. He wasn't even groaning. He was just lying very still.

'Is he dead?'

Brad leaned over him. 'I don't know,' he said and knelt down, putting his ear close to Sumo's mouth. 'He's not dead, I can hear him breathing.'

'Is he pretending to be dead?'

Brad pulled his eyelids back.

'No. He's unconscious. He'll probably come round in a few minutes. Come on. We'll put him in the locker room.'

Brad tipped the broken bits out of the black plastic bag and onto the floor. I wanted to say, 'What are you doing?' but I knew he was too busy to answer. I watched him twist the bag and make a kind of rope which he used to tie Sumo's hands behind his back. After that, we each grabbed hold of a foot and somehow, straining every muscle, we dragged him into the changing room. He was so heavy that it was like moving a giant whale.

That done, we went back into the corridor, picked up the broken pieces of the cistern and hid them behind a locker. We weren't going to leave a trail for anyone to follow.

'He'll yell the place down when he wakes up,' I said. 'How are we going to keep him quiet?'

Brad picked up the helmet. 'This should do it. You can't talk through these things, believe me. These are for protection not communication.'

He struggled to pull the helmet over the head of the unconscious man, then he closed the visor so that his face was completely hidden. It was obvious that, with his hands tied, he wouldn't be able to remove it. Good thinking, Brad.

'Your overall,' I said. 'Take it off. Leave it here. You'll be as easy to spot as a rabbit's tail in a ploughed field.'

'I guess so,' he said, pulling down the zip which ran from his chin and over his stomach. He tugged the suit off his shoulders and wriggled until he was able to wrench it over his jeans. As he held up the suit, I saw letters stencilled on the back: DR X FRANKWALL. They weren't quite as big as I had expected but black letters on white were still pretty noticeable.

When Brad spotted them, he was shocked. 'What the . . . ?'

'So you didn't know what was written on your back?'

'No way.'

'And nobody saw?'

'They couldn't have or I'd be mincemeat. I just followed them into the lab – remember the one with the eggs? I was the last to go in so I guess nobody saw my back.'

He hung the outfit on the hook.

'Right. Let's go!' I said and we raced towards the side door. I opened it and checked there was no one around. Then we fled across the compound but, as we did, the vultures started up squawking and making a terrible din. They were wasting their breath. Nobody would take any notice. The men were all too busy.

We raced onto the hillside. We ran without stopping and soon my lungs were burning and my muscles were screaming for me to rest. When I tripped and fell sprawling full length on the ground, all I wanted to do was to stay there breathing the sweet smell of the heather and go to sleep. I closed my eyes. My chest was heaving up and down, but Brad wouldn't let me stay.

'You've got to get up, Ally. Come on. Once they find Sumo, they'll start looking for us. Then we'll be in real trouble.'

I struggled to my feet, knowing he was right. We had to go. I told myself we were on the final leg of our mission. In less than an hour – half an hour, maybe – we'd be back at the cave.

We were almost at the steps that led down to the beach and I was beginning to feel safe again. My feet, which had been as heavy as lead for the past half-hour, suddenly felt light as I ran over those last few metres. But before we reached the steps we suddenly heard stomach-churning screeching above us. We looked up and saw the vultures, huge and black against the sky, circling overhead. They had appeared out of nowhere, like a formation of deadly war planes.

I froze on the spot, my mouth open. I knew for certain that they were going to attack us. But vultures didn't attack, did they? How come these...?

'Keep going,' Brad yelled. 'Stay low and cover your head.'

I ran forward with my knees bent, pulling my sweater over my head which made it difficult to see anything except my feet. The birds dived. I felt one pass my ear. I felt the wing of another strike my back. I screamed.

'Don't slow down, Ally. We're nearly there.'

As I peeped out to check where I was going, I saw the biggest, most terrifying bird flying towards me, its hooked beak wide open, ready to strike. There was no doubt that I was its target. I darted sideways, the vulture missing me by millimetres, but I stumbled and fell off balance, landing on the grass in a crumpled heap. I struggled to get to my feet but I was too slow. A second one, hardly smaller than the first, was following on and coming towards me. It was diving straight at me. I was helpless. I curled up tight, my hands over my head, waiting to feel it tear into my skin.

Chapter Twenty-Two

The vulture's beak ripped into my back. Only the thickness of my clothes saved me from serious injury but the bird had shredded my sweater, leaving my skin open to the next attack. Another vulture was heading my way.

It was Brad who saved me. He aimed a piece of rock at the bird which struck its wing, so that it was knocked off course and missed its target again. It flapped past me, squawking angrily. But, before it could turn and try again, Brad grabbed my hand and pulled me to my feet.

'RUN!' he yelled, pushing me towards the steps while he picked up more stones.

I ran on and, before the birds could attack, I reached the steps and hurried, scrambling and slipping, until I was halfway down the cliff. Gasping for breath, I stopped and pressed my back against the rock face. It would be almost impossible for the vultures to lunge at me without crashing into it. For the moment, I was safe.

I stood waiting, trying to recover my breath and I looked up to the top of the cliff. The vultures were circling again, their enormous black wings silhouetted against the sky. They were preparing to swoop. But where was Brad? Why hadn't he followed me?

One by one, the birds dived and I heard Brad scream. I started to run back to help him but, before I got to the top, Brad appeared, taking a flying leap then sliding and bumping down the steps until he reached me. He looked terrible. His sweater was shredded and soaked in blood. So were his face and arms. And there was a huge gash across his cheek.

'How did you get away?'

He sat on the step, his mouth open, gasping for air.

'I grabbed large stones,' he told me when he had got his breath back. 'I hurled them as the vultures swooped. I missed most of them but I managed to hit one. It was dead for sure. I guess the others will feed off their brother's flesh and pick his bones clean. They won't be interested in us now they've got their dinner.'

'I don't understand why they came after us,' I said. 'Vultures eat dead flesh. They don't attack the living.'

'It's pretty strange to me, too, Ally. But Dracula

and his team can do crazy things – so maybe they trained those birds to attack. If they can create storms, who's to say they can't breed a vulture that kills?'

We heard nothing more of the birds. Brad wiped off some of the blood and we walked down the steps and onto the beach. I was first to reach the cave.

'Ally!' Kim shouted. 'I've been out of my mind with worry. Where the hell did you go? And where's Brad?'

Brad was right behind me. His mum grabbed him by the shoulders and shook him. 'You stupid, stupid boy! Never do that again. Never. Why did you do it? Why?' Then she suddenly crumpled and started to sob. She flung her arms round his neck and hugged him for so long that I thought he might faint through lack of air. Lizzie went wild and Kirstie came over and hugged me, too, but it was a friendly, sisterly kind of hug that felt nice but wasn't too yucky. It was good.

Kim made a big fuss about all the blood, of course. 'Look at you! What on earth happened?' she said, but before we could explain she had hurried away to get some stuff to clean us up.

Richard was sitting on a rock and looking much

better than when we had left. 'You didn't go over to that laboratory, did you?' he asked us. 'Tell me you didn't.'

I pulled out the disc. 'Got the data.'

His jaw dropped.

'You did what?'

'She got the data from their computer, Dad,' Brad said.

Kim came back, carrying a bottle of antiseptic, and overheard him. 'You're kidding! You didn't, did you?'

I nodded.

'How?'

'She's a genius, that's what,' said Brad. 'But one of the men spotted us and we had to get out in a hurry.'

Kim looked anxious again. 'Were you guys followed?'

The picture of the Sumo Wrestler tied up in the changing room flashed across my mind. 'No,' I said. 'Nobody followed us. Just a few vultures, that's all.'

I don't think they took that last bit seriously. All they wanted to know was what we'd found out.

'They've been using the island as a trial,' I told them. 'Using some kind of mega-powerful device for creating storms. They destroyed everything here. But they're moving on.'

'We heard them talking,' said Brad. 'They're planning to strike the mainland.'

Kim's face looked grey and serious. 'These storms they create could bring on earthquakes and bring huge cities into chaos.'

'We must go to the police as soon as we get to the mainland,' Kirstie suggested.

'No,' said Brad. 'Frankwall has developed this weapon and he's about to sell it to anyone who can pay. His men have probably infiltrated the police.'

Kim nodded. 'Then we take the disc to the Parliament Building in Edinburgh.'

'It was closed last year,' I said. 'There were several terrorist attacks and the government decided that Edinburgh Castle was safer.'

'I hadn't realised,' she said. 'Very well. We'll take the disc to the castle and tell them what we have seen. Those in power will decide what to do next.'

'There's one thing,' said Brad. 'We overheard Frankwall say that they were having problems on the mainland. People were asking questions about Shairn. I reckon they told them a pack of lies about what was happening here.'

'Dad would never believe anything those people told him,' Kirstie said. 'He's not stupid.'

'Unless,' said Richard, 'they were dressed as police or said they were government officials.'

'Right,' said Kim. 'Then I suggest we find your dad so that he can tell us what's been going on. As soon as the light begins to fade, we'll set sail.'

But I was worried about being seen. 'We mustn't go into Balfour harbour. Frankwall's men are probably there, too, and on the lookout. If we land there, they'll know where we came from and we'll be finished.'

'There's a small inlet further down the coast,' Kirstie said. 'Grandad took me there in his rowing boat once. We could anchor there. No one will see us and we can walk over the hill to the bothy where Grandad's staying.'

'OK,' Kim said. 'Good plan. Let's do it. First, we load the boat.'

'Is Dad OK to go?'

'He's made a great recovery thanks to the medicines we carry.' She put her hand on his shoulder and smiled. 'He's going to be fine.'

Kirstie sat with Richard while the rest of us carried the things out of the cave. We rolled our jeans up above the knee and waded through the shallows to load the boat. I was really looking forward to the trip. The boat was plenty big enough for five of us and would be pure luxury after living in a ruined cottage and a rat-infested chapel. There were even seats with cushions on. It occurred to me that there might be a shower – I was beginning to smell – but I didn't ask. Having smelly armpits isn't all that important compared with saving the world. That's what I think, anyway.

The night was totally dark by the time we left the cave for the final time and we had to use torches to find our way down the beach. Leaning on Kim, Richard managed to walk out with us.

Only Kirstie hung back. 'Nobody's thought about Dobbin, have they? What happens to him?'

Brad was brilliant. He explained that a horse would be able to survive. 'He'll easily find grass and water. And when we've sorted things out we'll come back for him. Don't worry, Kirstie. He'll be fine. He's a tough old boy.'

Lizzie trotted behind us on three legs and Kirstie was walking really well, too. Kim had strapped on a special plastic boot which supported her foot so that there was only a hint of a limp.

At the edge of the water, Brad gave Kirstie a piggy back to the boat and even Richard was able to wade out and climb on board. The four of us sat on plastic benches in the cockpit while Kim, who was skipper, stood at the wheel. There were so many dials and instruments that it looked more like the control panel of a plane than a boat.

'OK crew!' she called to us. 'Here we go! Half an hour or so and we'll be on the mainland.'

We felt the excitement as she turned the key – we were on our way!

We waited for the sound of the engine but there was nothing more than a grinding noise. Kim tried once more . . . and again . . . with the same result.

I remembered then how Kirstie had tried to start Robbie Roberts' car abandoned by the harbour in Caitlin. That car had looked perfectly fine but there had been the same grinding noise. When I thought about it, nothing had worked since the storm. No lights, watches, cameras, telephones. Nothing. Only Frankwall's lab was in working order. Apart from that, all the electrics on the island had been fried.

Now the boat was dead in the water.

Chapter Twenty-Three

Kim was furious. 'I'll think of some way out of this. We're going to get off this island – I promise.'

I hoped she wasn't going to suggest floating to the mainland on a plank of wood. The Atlantic Ocean was freezing cold even in summer and I didn't fancy landing on the shore as a block of ice. I'd rather go back to the cave and wait for someone to rescue us.

I made this suggestion but it went down like a lead balloon.

'So how are we going to get out of here?' Kirstie asked.

'Marine biologists aren't totally reliant on engine power and electronic equipment.'

'What then?'

'There's the dinghy.'

She explained that sometimes, when they wanted to investigate an area where it might be tricky for the big boat, they would take the dinghy. 'You'd be surprised how often we use it.'

Kim and Brad pulled on long waterproof boots and jumped into the water. Then the rest of us shone torches so they could see. The dinghy was fixed on the back of the boat and just needed to be untied and floated round to the front ready to take it out to sea.

'This is not going to be so comfortable – but we'll manage. It'll take five of us...'

'...and Lizzie.'

'Yes, of course. And the dog. We can all take turns to row. Can you row, Alexandra?'

'Sure,' I said.

Once in the dinghy, she handed me two oars so I gave a demonstration of my impressive rowing technique. I didn't mean to hit Kirstie. I was only showing how well I could row. But somehow I knocked her and she sort of...fell. I didn't do it on purpose. Honest.

'You are just so careless!' she yelled and she was really horrible to me. The others understood it was an accident – but not my sister. So what's new?

'We'll be rowing for at least an hour so we'd better take it in turns. I'll go first to get us clear of the shore.'

When we were ready for off, Brad held up his hands and said, 'Hold on! Let me go and get my kite surfer. I'll help us along. The wind's blowing in the right direction.'

Richard said, 'Smart thinking, son.' and Kim agreed that it was a good idea.

Brad came back from the boat with a bundle under his arm. He unfolded the kite and spread it out. It was awesome.

'Wow! I've never seen a kite as big as that.'

'That's why I thought it would help. It's a bit like the sail of a yacht.'

I'd seen kite surfers on telly but never the real thing. Brad showed me how it worked.

'I buckle this strap round my waist, see. The kite's fixed to it by these long strings which I can pull to control the direction – the way you control some of the bigger kites. You can make them go pretty much any way you want them to.'

I was getting the idea.

'Usually, I'd be standing on the board with my feet fixed in slots and being pulled over the waves by the kite – it's a great sport. It's a bit like windsurfing but with a kite.'

'Don't you get blown off course? Isn't it dangerous?'

'Yeah, it can be. You just have to be real careful.'

I could see that we would move much faster with the sail pulling, too. The oars alone would move the boat along but it would be slow.

'Brad,' Kim said, 'I want you to wait until we're away from the shore before you use the kite.'

She settled into the rower's seat and pulled away until rounding the headland and going towards the mainland – which was visible only when the moon crept from behind the bank of heavy cloud.

Brad had fixed the belt around his waist and attached the control lines that held the kite. He was waiting for the word.

'I'm ready. Shall I release it, Mom?'

'No. Wait,' she said and handed the oars to me. 'Take over, please, Ally. I'm going to hang onto Brad. If this wind gets up he could be pulled overboard.'

Brad wasn't pleased. 'Oh, Mom. Don't fuss. Of course I won't. The wind will pull the dinghy faster, that's all.'

But she insisted.

Brad released the kite slowly. It was too dark to see properly but we could hear the canvas flapping above our heads. It filled with the wind and I could feel the dinghy pull away like a sports car at the starting blocks.

'That's fantastic, Brad,' I yelled as I pulled on the

oars. 'We'll be on the mainland in no time.'

We were well away from the island when the wind became stronger, whipping up the waves. They began to batter the dinghy, rocking it violently from side to side so that we had to hang on with both hands or we would have been swept overboard. Lizzie, unable to keep her feet, slid from one end to the other until Kirstie caught her with her foot and trapped her between her knees to keep her safe.

'The sea around these parts is quite often wild,' Kim yelled over the noise of the waves. 'We'll just have to get through it.'

We were soon soaked to the skin. But things were worse up front for Brad. The wind became so strong that it was almost pulling him out of the boat.

'Release the belt, Brad,' Kim shouted. 'Let the kite go.'

He began to unfasten the buckle – but there was something wrong. 'I can't get it to open up,' he called back.

The wind was tearing at him as he continued to fiddle with the buckle. I handed my oar to Kirstie and went to help.

'We'll have to cut the lines,' Kim yelled. 'It's the only way. Richard, have you got your knife?'

He hadn't.

'It's in the boat. I left in the tool box.'

Then I remembered Grandad's Swiss army knife. 'I've got one,' I shouted. 'It's in my pocket.'

I tried to take it out but it was difficult to keep my balance as the dinghy thrashed about in the stormy sea and I was flung onto the bottom. I flailed about in the wet until I somehow managed to grab hold of Kim. Pounded by the waves, I held onto her with one hand and reached into my pocket with the other. I was shaking with cold but I finally pulled the knife out and reached forward to pass it to Kim.

'You hold onto Brad, Ally,' she shouted. 'I'll cut him loose.'

The lines holding the kite were wet and my knife was not as sharp as it might be. Kim sawed at the ropes while I held Brad against the powerful pull of the wind. Again and again she sawed, determined to cut through. But they resisted the blade.

I held Brad as best I could but my arms began to weaken and, although I tried to lock my fingers together round Brad's waist, they were wet and slippery and I was in danger of letting him go.

Kim kept on trying. She sawed until her hand must have cramped from gripping the knife. Still she didn't give up until finally the lines broke one by one and the kite flew free. Then Brad fell back onto the bottom of the dinghy, exhausted.

Chapter Twenty-Four

The storm continued until we were weak from holding onto the dinghy. The temptation to close my eyes and let go was very strong – even though I would be swept overboard if I did. Somehow, I kept a grip and so did everybody else. Kim had taken over the oars. She tried to keep rowing but was helpless against the power of the ocean and so she gave up and leaned forward, resting on the oars.

'Best to wait for the storm to blow itself out,' Richard said. 'The wind's weakening. I can definitely feel it, can't you?'

Kim agreed with him. 'The waves are smaller and I'm sure the swell isn't as strong.'

The waves still looked as high as mountains to me – but then who am I to argue with a marine biologist? I'm just a girl with a certificate for a hundred metres breaststroke and a rosette for catching the most crabs on Lillicombe beach. Tides, storms and ocean currents are not my strong point.

Kim and Richard were right. Soon, the wind dropped and the waves calmed so that we were able to sit in the dinghy without holding on for dear life.

'I'm not sure where we are,' Kim said. 'We were tossed around so much, I don't know where north is anymore.' She looked up into the sky. 'The old mariners sailed around the world long ago using the North Star for their guide. They would take a fix on it. So you see, when all your equipment fails, there's always a star to guide you.'

But not that night. The storm had left the sky so covered in cloud that few stars were visible.

'None of them is the North Star,' Richard said. 'The North Star is strong and bright. There's no mistaking it. We'll wait until it gets light and then we'll be able to see where we are.'

We prepared to do nothing until dawn. There was no point in rowing in the wrong direction. We didn't want to find ourselves halfway to America.

We clung together, dozing until the sky began to lighten and the sun crept over the horizon. I was first to open my eyes and see mainland Scotland in the distance.

I woke everyone by yelling, 'Land ahoy!' Kirstie and Brad seemed pleased but when Kim looked around, she was horrified.

'I don't believe it!' she yelled. 'Richard, look where we are.'

He looked equally shocked. 'Brad, take one of the oars. We need both of you. Quick as you can, son.'

'What's the panic?' asked Brad, scrambling to sit next to his mother.

'Look at the movement of the water. Do you see?'

Brad shielded his eyes from the sun and looked to the right. Then he turned and looked left. He had spotted something, I could tell – and whatever it was, he didn't like it.

'Now I see it,' he said and, sitting next to his mother, began to row frantically.

'What?' I said. 'All I can see is water. Miles and miles of it.'

'You know about whirlpools?'

'Yeah.'

Richard took up the explanation. 'That's one of the largest in these parts and it's drawing the dinghy towards it. They're going to have to row like crazy to get us away.'

It's difficult to keep your eyes fixed on a particular area of water but I tried. But the more I tried the more impossible it was. I kept imagining we were heading nearer the whirlpool. Then I thought we were getting further away. Kirstie was just as bad. She couldn't decide either. Nearer? Farther? We didn't know. But we were terrified of being drawn into the whirlpool and sucked into the water. We'd heard about ships that had been lost that way. Grandad had told us.

Kim and Brad rowed, gritting their teeth as they pulled on the oars – and the dinghy began to move away from the whirlpool – gradually, gradually. When they realised we were safe, they dropped their oars and flopped forward just like rowers do at the end of the Boat Race every year. They were gasping for breath and it was some time before they could speak.

'We're out of danger now,' Richard said. 'Well done, you two. Do you think you could row now, Ally? I'm only sorry my arm's out of action and I can't help.'

With the mainland in view, I took over the oars and Kirstie took over as lookout.

'Will you point out the inlet you mentioned,' Kim said. 'We want to avoid Balfour harbour, don't we?'

Kirstie said there was no problem. She knew the inlet very well and would take us right there.

'You've all been fantastic,' said Kim, which was quite a compliment as she and Brad had been the real heroes – like Olympic oarsmen. I thought they deserved a gold medal.

I rowed the dinghy, knowing that the coast of Scotland was coming nearer and nearer in the morning light. I thought about seeing Dad again and sitting by a fire in Grandad's bothy. Food featured strongly in this fantasy. Lots of it. Sausages, bacon, toast and chips. Lots and lots of chips. It felt good to me. It seemed like forever since I'd had a decent meal.

The sea was as calm as a millpond as we finally sailed into the shallow waters of the inlet. Kim, who was still wearing the rubber boots, jumped out and pulled the dinghy clear of the water and up onto a narrow shingle beach. We were well hidden from view and sat on some boulders, drinking from water bottles and eating the survival bars. We were like drowned rats. Exhausted, dirty, drowned rats at that.

We hid the dinghy near some rocks and set off to walk inland. Leaving the beach behind, we climbed the hill then skirted round Balfour so we wouldn't be seen. The day was warm and midges hovered round our heads. They were a real pest at this time of year. We had to carry pieces of bracken which we flapped to keep them away from our faces. It occurred to me then that there had been no midges on the island that summer. I should have noticed before. The midges, along with the birds, had disappeared.

We walked more slowly than usual, partly because of Kirstie's ankle and partly because we'd had no sleep and we were dog-tired. All except Lizzie who was a dog. Sometimes on that walk, I closed my eyes and I swear I fell asleep and still kept walking. We just had to keep going. Time was running out.

When we were well up the hill beyond Balfour, we joined the narrow road that linked the town with the major route to Fort William. We were grateful to be walking on tarmac. Hard as it was, it was so much easier than constantly lifting our feet over clumps of heather and bracken.

The road was quiet that day. Only once, towards the end of that stretch, did we see a car. Kirstie spotted it in the distance – a Land Rover heading towards us.

'Hide!' she screamed. 'Hide! Hide!'

She thought we should fling ourselves into the heather and lie low – but we were too slow and it was moving fast. We didn't have time.

'Let's not get paranoid,' Kim said. 'We're letting our imaginations run away with us.'

I didn't know what 'paranoid' was but if it was anything to do with panicking, my sister was paranoid with bells on.

We walked on up the narrow road – a bedraggled group of pilgrims on a journey to reach Grandad's bothy. For Kirstie and me, it had been a long, long journey – from the cottage, to the chapel and the lab and the cave – not to mention the stormy sea crossing. But we were nearly there now. Not far to go. Then we'd be safe.

When we finally left the road, we crossed the hill and the small stone building came into view.

'That's it!' I yelled and left the others and ran ahead – though I don't know how I found the energy. Then, well before I got there, the door of the bothy opened and Dad came racing over the heather to meet us.

'Ally! Kirstie!' he shouted. 'Oh thank goodness you're here. Thank goodness.'

When I reached him, I flung myself at him and threw my arms round his neck. Kirstie, who wasn't far behind in spite of her leg, did the same and there we were, hanging onto him for fear that he might turn out to be a mirage or a dream or a ghost. As long as we held on, we knew he was real.

When we dared to let go, I saw Grandad standing in the doorway, his white hair wild and unruly as it always was and his tufty eyebrows shielding his eyes that were crinkly from smiling.

'Come in, all of you,' he called. 'You'll be needing a rest, I've no doubt.'

All five of us (and Lizzie, of course) crowded into the square, stone-walled room that was kitchen, living room and bedroom rolled into one. It smelt of wood smoke but the simmering stew in the pot that rested on the fire was the best smell in the world. Grandad always had something in a pot no matter what time of day. Thank goodness.

'Sit yourselves down,' he said. 'You look as if you've had a terrible time of it.'

It was quite a squeeze in the bothy, but we sat on the bed and Dad made us take off our wet clothes and wrapped us in blankets. I put the disc we had taken from the lab on the top of a small cupboard for safety and went to the table where Grandad was ladling steaming beef and vegetables onto plates. I will never, never, never forget the taste of it – the meat, the tender leeks and carrots and potatoes and the thick brown gravy. It was the most delicious, perfect meal I had ever eaten – though I didn't know what to call it. Too late for breakfast. Too early for lunch. But we ate until we were full to bursting.

When we had finished and the clothes were drying nicely by the fire, we talked about the island – how scary things were going on, how Caitlin had been destroyed and what we'd found in the laboratory. Even the killer vultures.

'Did I no tell you something was going on?' said Grandad. 'But you wouldna listen, would you, Andrew? No! I was just a crazy old man. Imagining things.'

It was in the middle of this conversation that I heard a noise which set my heart pounding. Someone was a knocking at the door. It came so unexpectedly – out there, miles from anywhere. It terrified me. Who would come to the bothy? And why would they come? I stood up and went to the window. Not far away, out on the heather, a car was parked. Not just any car – it was the Land Rover that had passed us not half an hour ago. Had someone come for Grandad? I didn't think so. A knot tightened in my stomach which told me that someone had come for us.

Chapter Twenty-Five

Grandad stepped outside and shut the door behind him.

'Are you the owner of this place?' a man asked.

'Aye. Who's askin'?'

'We're the Medical Security Alert Team,' he said. 'We believe there are people around these parts who might have come from outside the area. You'll be aware that we are taking extra precautions owing to the outbreak of a serious virus on the Isle of Shairn.'

'Am I aware? Wheesht man, wasn't I at the meeting in the chapel hall two days ago? Didn't I have to listen to all that claptrap about National Security? Didn't I sign the Official Secrets Act like everybody else in Balfour? Of course I'm aware. I've got good reason to be aware. My grandchildren are over on the island.'

The man at the door coughed. 'We are taking special care of everyone, sir. A temporary hospital has been set up and no one's life is in danger.'

'And how long is this going on for? You've kept us in the dark long enough.'

'Just a few more days then you will be able to go

across to see them. Perhaps my colleague and I could come in and talk about it?'

Up until then, we had been sitting without moving, without making a noise and hoping they would stay outside. So when I heard those words, I wanted to be sick. After all we'd been through, it looked as if we were going to be caught, right here in Grandad's bothy.

But I needn't have panicked because Dad opened the window in the back wall and flapped his hand, beckoning us to come over. Grandad was stalling for time. He managed to keep them talking at the door while we all crept to the window and squeezed through. Once we were out, we ran across to an old stone wall which had probably been part of a sheep pen. We ducked down behind it to hide and even Lizzie seemed to know what to do. Remember – we were only wearing blankets and, what with the wind blowing and everything, we were freezing and shivering like mad as we waited for them to drive away.

Suddenly a thought struck me like a flash of electricity. Horror! If they did go into the bothy, the first thing they would spot would be the plates and spoons – five of them – on the kitchen table. They would be a dead giveaway, that's for sure.

'I'm going back,' I whispered to Dad. He tried to hold me but I slipped from his grasp and hared across to the window. I peeped in to check that the so-called Medical Team weren't inside, then I vaulted through. I began to clear the table without making a sound (which was very, very difficult – especially the spoons). I stuffed everything out of sight under the bed. I could hear Grandad still talking at the door and was about to climb back out of the window when I remembered our clothes hanging on the clotheshorse near the fire – how could I forget? I turned and started pulling them off but, as I did, the clotheshorse toppled and fell with a crash onto the stone floor making a terrible noise. That did it! They would be sure to come in now.

With the last of the clothes in my arms, I dived under the bed just in time to hear one of them say, 'I believe there's someone in there, sir. I think we should go in and look.'

The other man agreed. Grandad protested. There was a scuffle as good old Grandad tried to stop them but the door was flung back and they stormed in.

It was then that I remembered the disc. I'd put it on the cupboard when I got undressed. How stupid! Why hadn't I put it inside a cupboard? It was labelled FRANKWALL RESEARCH so, if those men saw it, we were finished. They would want to know why one of their discs was in the bothy. If they insisted on taking it, our evidence would be gone.

But all was not lost.

'Do you always treat other people's homes in this way?' It was Dad's voice! He must have come through the window. From my hiding place under the bed, I looked through a small hole in the sheet and I could see him sitting in the armchair as if he'd been there all along.

'These people are from the Medical Security Alert Team, Andrew.' It was Grandad speaking now. 'This is my son who is staying with me.'

The man cleared his throat. 'We have explained to your father that it is vitally important for national security that news of this outbreak does not leak out. A state of alert has been declared. Anyone passing on information will be classed as a spy and will be arrested.'

'You obviously don't know that I was at the meeting in Balfour,' said Dad. 'You don't seem very well informed. Haven't you got a list of names?'

The man turned to the other one and snapped, 'You have the list in the car?'

166

'Er, no, sir. It's back at the...er...office.'

'You're not doing your job very well, are you?' said Dad. 'This is supposed to be a national emergency. Why come bursting into my father's home? He's an old man. How can he be a threat?'

They both blushed with embarrassment.

'I apologise for the intrusion, sir, but we saw a suspicious group of people on the road just now.'

'Well,' said Grandad. 'I don't know where you think I might be hiding anyone in this wee place but I suggest you go back and tell them that you didn't find any aliens in my bothy. Unless they're up the chimney, of course. Would you like to look? But mind the soot. I'd hate you to get it on your clean uniforms.'

The two men muttered something then the door banged shut and the engine of the Land Rover started up as they drove away.

I poked my head out from under the bed. 'Cool, Grandad,' I said as I scrambled from under the bed. 'They didn't see the disc, did they? Tell me they didn't.'

I looked over to the cupboard but it was gone.

'Don't worry, Ally,' Dad said. 'I've got it safe. I'll look after it. We can't afford to lose that data now.'

'No, Dad. I want it.'

'You know this is evidence,' he said, pulling the disc from his pocket.

'Yes, of course I know! Why is it because I'm a kid you think I can't look after it? I broke into the laboratory, didn't I? I copied the data off the computer!'

'Yes but . . .'

'If I can do that, Dad, I think I can take care of the disc.'

He nodded and handed it back to me and I hugged him to show how glad I was to have it.

'You don't think those people will come back, do you?' I said.

Grandad winked. 'We'll wait a wee while, sweetheart. But dinnae fash yerrsel. We'll be all right now.'

I pulled all the clothes out from under the bed. They were almost dry and I put mine on. After that, the three of us sat and listened and, when we had heard nothing, Dad went out of the door as if he was off for a walk. I watched him through the window, strolling up to a high point, checking to see if our visitors were still around. When all was clear, he hurried down to the stone wall to tell the others that they could come out of hiding. The coast was clear. They must have turned blue out there without their clothes, so they didn't have to be asked twice before they ran back inside. Then we all had plenty to say.

We talked some more about the lab at Tarbay and I described Dracula in detail.

'His real name was Dr Frankwall,' I said. 'He was really horrible and spooky.'

'Did you say Frankwall?' Grandad asked. 'He was at the meeting in Balfour. He told us all about a virus and how we mustn't make contact outside the area. He even took everybody's mobiles. He seemed like a very clever man.'

'It was a pack of lies, of course,' said Dad. 'He's fooled so many people.'

'I reckon he's in control of everything,' I said. 'At that laboratory, they're somehow able to control the weather.'

'Nothing would work on Shairn,' said Kirstie. 'Not lights or cars or phones. Not even watches. How did they do that?'

'It's something to do with those storms, I guess,' said Richard. 'They've wiped out all the electrics on the island.'

'Then how come the Men in Black were travelling

around in the APC?' Kirstie asked. 'That was working OK.'

'If they kept it in a specially protected garage while the storm was raging, it wouldn't be affected,' Kim explained. 'Did you notice that the lab had an unusual coating on the building?'

'Yes. A sort of white plastic.'

'That was probably designed to give similar protection so that the computers wouldn't be affected.'

Dad shook his head. 'And all their clever experiments have wiped out a whole village and killed the islanders.'

'That's terrible indeed,' Grandad said. 'It's like a weapon of mass destruction and they could terrorise us all – if they get the chance.'

'We've got to do something,' I said. 'They're moving to the mainland.'

'It's important that we get away from here,' Kim insisted. 'We all know far too much. If any one of us is caught, we're finished.'

It was true. We were surrounded by dangerous people who would kill us without a second thought.

'We must tell someone in power what's going on,' said Richard.

Grandad nodded. 'I agree. We have to save the world from these terrible people.'

'We need to get to Edinburgh as soon as possible,' Kirstie said. 'We'll take the disc to the Scottish Parliament. They'll take notice of us.'

Dad looked at Grandad. And Grandad looked at Dad.

'At the moment, that's almost impossible,' said Grandad. 'For one thing, I've no car. Or are you planning to walk all the way to Edinburgh?'

'You must know somebody who would lend us one.'

'Oh aye. I do. But that wouldn't do you any good.'

'Why not?'

'There are roadblocks, lassie. Nobody is allowed in or out of Balfour until the so-called crisis on Shairn is at an end. That's what they told us. I've seen the roadblocks with my own eyes and I know people have been turned back.'

We sat in the bothy in silence. Thinking. All seven of us – and Lizzie – thinking. Somehow, we had to find a way of getting to Edinburgh before Dr Frankwall did his worst. We had to tell them what we had seen on the island and give them the disc.

We had to.

Chapter Twenty-Six

After all that thinking, it was Grandad who came up with the idea of borrowing a horse and cart.

'There's a track that would take us over the hills. It meets up with the road to Lochailort and I don't suppose those bird brains even know the track exists. A horse and cart will get us as far as Lochailort and from there we can catch the train.'

'But you haven't got a horse and cart, Grandad.'

He scratched his head. 'Nor I have! Well would you believe it!' Then he grinned. 'I haven't got a cart but Rab MacGillicuddy has.'

'Will he lend it to us?'

'He'll be more than willing to lend it, I reckon. He doesn't like this situation any more than we do. He doesn't like being told what to do by a bunch of ninnies.'

The plan was that I should go to the MacGillicuddys' farm, about a mile away, where Rab and his family lived.

'I'll write a letter explaining what's going on. You can walk over there and take Lizzie with you. If anyone sees you, they won't think anything of a girl taking her dog for a romp, will they?'

Grandad sat down and wrote the letter and I put it in my pocket.

'And what after I've given it to him?'

'I've asked Rab to meet us at the cart track near here. He'll signal when he's leaving by lighting his fire – it's all in the letter, lassie. He'll know what to do. We'll see the smoke from the chimney, no problem. If things should go wrong, you come straight back here. All right, hen?'

Everyone wished me luck and slapped me on the back and I felt like Scott of the Antarctic about to leave on a perilous journey. I was only going to the MacGillicuddys' farm, for goodness sake. It wasn't exactly wild and dangerous territory. We set out, Lizzie and me, walking across the hill. My clothes were dry, the day was warmer now and I was feeling good. It was such a normal thing to do – taking my dog for a walk. There hadn't been too many normal things in the past few days. Normal. Ordinary. Regular. Average. Common. Routine. No. My life had been none of those things lately.

I kept my eyes open as I strolled across the heather and up the hillside. I watched for any sign of movement, any sign of people – but there was nothing. When I finally came to the brow of the hill, I looked down to see the farm below me, pressed close to the hillside, protected from the prevailing wind, and I ran all the way down. Lizzie ran with me, barking.

Mrs MacGillicuddy was in the farmyard.

'Well, wee lassie. And where might you be going?' she called.

When I'd caught my breath, I told her why I'd come and I gave her the letter.

'I'll call Rab. He's away in the field.'

She went to the fence, cupped her hands round her mouth and shouted to a man on the far side. He looked up from the fence he was mending but didn't move until she shouted again and beckoned him to come in. He started to walk towards us but came at a pace that suggested he wasn't in any mood to hurry.

'What is it, woman?' Rab MacGillicuddy called as he came nearer. 'I have work to do. Why have you called me?'

'This lassie's brought you a letter from Angus. You'd better come inside.'

'Angus, you say? And why would he be writing me letters?'

The three of us sat round the kitchen table while

Rab MacGillicuddy unfolded the paper and read it. We watched as he held the letter close to his face and read it very slowly, moving his lips as if saying the words to himself. When he had finished, he thumped his fist on the table and roared.

'Heaven save us! I knew there was something going on. Those men didn't look right. There was something strange about them. I said so from the start, didn't I, Margaret?' He looked at me and grinned. 'Well, they'll have the MacGillicuddys to contend with now. We've beaten better men than that crowd of Sassenachs. Of course you shall have the cart, lassie. Of course! And I've two fine horses to pull it. Had them ten years or more. Raised them myself, I did.'

Mrs MacGillicuddy laughed. 'If they weren't so big, you'd think they were his babies.'

'Aye. Fine beasts. Fine beasts. They've won prizes, so they have. They'll no let us down.'

'Are you coming with us, Mr MacGillicuddy?'

'Aye. You'll be needing me to drive the cart, lassie.'

'There's one thing,' said Mrs MacGillicuddy. 'The cart track swings near to the Balfour road at one point – not far from the roadblock, in fact. You could be spotted by the guards. A horse and cart isn't easy to hide.'

'Aye, you're right, woman,' Rab MacGillicuddy said as he leaned back in his chair and sucked his teeth.

'Do we have to go on that cart track?' I asked. 'Couldn't we just go over the hill?'

He shook his head. 'You'd never get the cart across the heather. No. The only thing to do is leave the cart and ride the horses. You'll have to leave the cart here.'

'There are seven of us and we all need to get away. We need to talk to the authorities in Edinburgh. But the horses can't carry seven of us.'

Silence again. Heavy sighs. Lots of thinking.

Then Mrs MacGillicuddy had a brainwave. 'I'll take the car up to the roadblock and create a diversion.'

'A diversion? What do you mean, Margaret? Are you mad?'

'Not at all. I shall drive up to the roadblock and pretend I'd forgotten all about the ban on leaving Balfour. Then I'll tell them a story about my Aunt Janet in Fort William who is very old and has a heart condition and how I go to see her every week.'

'What good will that do?'

'Oh, I can spin the story out for as long as you like. They'll have their attention on me while you go past in the cart. The car engine will be running so there'll be a deal of noise to cover any that the cart makes.'

Mr MacGillicuddy wasn't so sure. 'What if they won't listen to your story? What if they tell you to go back?'

'Then I shall stall the car, Rab. That old thing stalls at the blink of an eye. I'll pretend to be a helpless woman and ask the guards to look under the bonnet and try and get it going – or they can push me all the way home, whichever they choose.'

Mr MacGillicuddy laughed. 'I think you've come up with a good plan, Margaret. Aye, a good plan.'

Mrs MacGillicuddy lit the fire in the grate, sending a plume of smoke up the chimney while I helped Mr MacGillicuddy to harness the horses to the cart. It was a large wooden farm cart – probably very old – with huge wooden wheels. I had never ridden in one before and I was surprised how high up we were. I could see for miles.

Mr MacGillicuddy flicked the reins and the horses moved off down the drive. His wife followed in the car – an old banger which had once been red but was now faded and edged with rust. At the gate, the cart turned left up a narrow track while the car turned right, to join the road that led out of Balfour. We were on our way.

Before long, we had reached the spot where we had arranged to meet Grandad. Sure enough – there he was, lying in the bracken by the side of the cart track. It was his white hair that gave him away. He should have worn a woolly hat or something. He'd never make a spy! When I peered more closely, I saw the rest of the group nearby, all well hidden. One by one, Mr MacGillicuddy helped them into the cart. Nobody spoke. Sometimes, sounds can travel far across the hills and we didn't want to give the guards any hint that we were nearby. Everyone sat on the floor of the cart, hidden by the high wooden sides. I stayed up front. So did Lizzie.

We soon came to the spot where the track came within half a mile of the roadblock. This might sound a long way away, but the cart would be easily visible as it passed. We kept our fingers crossed that Mrs M would be there with her car, distracting the guards.

She was.

We saw that the bonnet of the old car was up and the two guards were bending over, looking into the engine. She had obviously decided not to tell the long story of her Aunt Janet's ailments. Mrs M was sitting in the driver's seat and must have had her foot on the accelerator because it was making a terrible noise. There was no danger that they would hear the horses' hooves or the wheels of the cart. In fact, the noise of the engine was so loud that they wouldn't have heard a dozen elephants walk past or a squadron of fighter jets fly over. Mrs M had done a great job. Mr MacGillicuddy turned and gave his passengers the thumbs-up.

It was only when we had reached the road to Lochailort that we felt we had really escaped and could start making plans for what we would do in Edinburgh.

Chapter Twenty-Seven

We had been going for an hour with Mr MacGillicuddy keeping us entertained with stories of Bonnie Prince Charlie. 'He came from France and he landed in secret on the coast not far from here.'

The stories were new to Brad and he thought they were cool. 'Did Charlie become king?' he asked when he had listened to several.

'No, laddie. He did not. He was finally beaten by the English at Culloden. A foul deed. Aye. A foul deed.'

The stories over, Grandad suggested we stopped for some food. 'It's half past one,' he said. 'Time we had a break, Rab.'

Mr MacGillicuddy pulled up outside a pub called The Bell. We climbed down and walked into the front room which smelled of wood smoke and beer and cigarettes.

'What can you rustle up for these folk, Alistair?' Mr MacGillicuddy called to the landlord who was standing behind the bar reading the paper. He looked up as we came in but he didn't look pleased to see us – even though the pub was empty.

'You've got children with you, I see,' he said.

'Aye. But you won't turn us away, will you, Alistair? We're as hungry as a flock of gannets.'

'I've nothing but cheese sandwiches. Take it or leave it, Rab.'

'Then I'll take it. Sandwiches all round. And while you're at it, five beers and three orange juices, if you please.'

The landlord shouted instructions over his shoulder, 'Cheese sandwiches for eight, Fiona.' He rested his paper on the bar, turned to the pumps and started pulling the pints of beer. As he pushed the drinks across the bar, he glanced out of the window.

'What in blue blazes are you doing out here with that old cart of yours?' he said as he opened the bottle of orange juice. 'Has your car broken down?'

Mr MacGillicuddy tapped the side of his nose and winked. 'I've got a real tale for you, Alistair.' And he leaned on the bar and told the whole story (plus one or two exaggerations). He told of the military patrol around Balfour, how we'd escaped the roadblock and how we were taking important information to Edinburgh.

'I don't believe a word of it,' the landlord said,

putting the last of the drinks on the bar. 'You and your tales.'

Mr MacGillicuddy was taken aback. 'And why not?'

'It's ridiculous. Whoever heard of such a thing? Ach, you're making it up, you silly old fool.'

'Making it up, indeed! Ask any of these good people. They'll tell you whether I'm making it up. We're off to the station in Lochailort so they can catch the train.'

'To Cloud Cuckoo Land?'

'To Edinburgh, I'll have you know, to present their findings to the Parliament.' He took a long swallow of his beer. 'This is of national importance.'

The landlord threw his head back and laughed. 'National importance, indeed! I've never heard such poppycock. Away with you.'

By then, Mr MacGillicuddy's face was red with fury. He slammed his glass on the bar and said, 'Poppycock, is it? No. I'll prove it. Alexandra. Show him the disc.'

The rest of us were feeling uncomfortable. 'Rab, that's enough,' Grandad protested. 'Leave well alone and come and sit down.'

'No. I'm not being called an old fool and a liar. I

won't stand for it. Go on, show him, lassie. Let him see the disc.'

Reluctantly, I took it out and held it for the landlord to look at.

He wasn't impressed. 'What does that prove? A CD? It proves nothing. NOTHING.'

Mr MacGillicuddy was steaming with rage. 'Another pint,' he demanded, pushing his empty glass across to the landlord. 'And hurry up with those sandwiches. We haven't got time to hang around.'

The sandwiches soon arrived but the atmosphere in the bar was as cold as Ben Nevis in December. No words passed between the landlord and Mr MacGillicuddy except just before we left when he had to pay the bill.

'That's daylight robbery!' he said.

'And how so?'

'You're asking a king's ransom for a few drinks and some stale sandwiches.'

'A king's ransom? I'm surprised you think so, Rab MacGillicuddy. People involved in national affairs aren't usually tight with their money.'

Mr M stood there defiantly, pulled out his wallet and slapped a single note on the bar. 'That'll have to do,' he said. 'I'm no payin' any more.'

The landlord went wild. 'That's not nearly enough, you old fraud.'

'It's as much as you're getting,' shouted Mr M.

The landlord raised his fist but – before a serious fight could break out – Grandad grabbed hold of Mr MacGillicuddy and dragged him out of the pub and into the cart, while the landlord ran after him, waving his fist and shouting, 'I'll have the law on you – you see if I don't. You owe me money, you old goat!'

But Mr M was already in his seat, wildly flicking the reins so that the cart moved off before the landlord could stop it.

Dad sat up front next to him, trying to calm his terrible temper and I had to sit on the floor of the cart between Brad and Kirstie. Every rut and stone made the cart bounce and we jerked about like rag dolls. I would have given my best fossil collection for a cushion.

'How long have we got before we get to Lochailort, Mr MacGillicuddy?' I called out. I was hoping he would say, 'Not more than ten minutes.' But he didn't.

'An hour at least, Alexandra. We'll have to see how we go.'

This wasn't good news as my bum was already

sore and I think we were all too tired to talk. One by one, we shut our eyes and dozed off.

What eventually woke us was the noise of a helicopter overhead.

'That's unusual in these parts,' Grandad said. 'Could be the RAF training, I suppose.'

Dad shook his head. 'That's not an RAF chopper.'

I thought it might be an air ambulance. 'Maybe there's been an accident.'

'No,' said Mr MacGillicuddy. 'It's more likely bringing some wealthy businessman up from London for a week's shooting.'

The helicopter was the only bit of excitement we had on a journey that seemed to last for ever. It was four o' clock before we arrived in Lochailort and Mr MacGillicuddy did a great job in pulling up right outside the station. There were a few heads turned when they saw the wooden cart. But we didn't care. We climbed down and said goodbye. Then we walked into the station and bought our tickets for Edinburgh.

'You're only just in time,' said the woman behind the glass as we passed her the money. 'You'll have to run if you're going to catch the four minutes past. There won't be another one for a wee while.'

As we hurried towards the platform, I turned to wave to Mr MacGillicuddy and was surprised to see that two men were standing in front of him, shouting. They looked very angry but Mr MacGillicuddy looked just as angry and was shouting back at them. I had no idea what the argument was about but, when I saw a policeman walking towards them I knew that, whatever was going on, he would sort it out.

We jumped on the train seconds before the doors closed. There were seats for all of us and Lizzie curled up underneath and slept all the way. The seats were brilliant – very soft and squidgy. They were the most comfortable seats I'd sat on in days and my poor bottom was almost purring with pleasure. I must have fallen asleep again because, when I woke up and looked at my watch, it was eight o' clock.

'Are we there yet?' I asked.

'We get into Glasgow at quarter to nine,' said Dad.

'Glasgow?'

'We change at Glasgow. It'll take an hour from there to Edinburgh.'

I sighed and went back to sleep hoping that the trip would be worth it. It was getting boring.

When we finally climbed out at Glasgow Central, the platforms were buzzing with people and most of them seemed to be boarding the Edinburgh train. It was so busy that we couldn't get seats close together. We were split up and had to take seats where we could. Brad and his parents were two carriages away from us. But we all agreed that we'd meet up on the platform at Waverley Station in an hour's time.

The train set off and we left Glasgow behind. I felt happy that we would soon be in Edinburgh – that is until I saw Brad walk into our carriage looking chalk-faced as if he'd seen a ghost.

'What's up?'

He glanced over his shoulder then leaned forward to speak. 'He's on the train, Ally. I saw him walking towards the front staring at people, as if he was looking for someone.'

'Who?'

'That man, Trudor. The one in charge of the lab. The one with the red hair.'

'Brush Head?' I sat up feeling alarmed at the news. 'Is he by himself?'

'No. The Sumo Wrestler's with him. They're both on the train and I'm certain they're looking for us.'

Chapter Twenty-Eight

Dad was sitting with Kirstie, three seats behind. When they saw Brad and me walking towards them, they knew that something had happened.

I leaned over and spoke in a low voice. 'Dad, I've got something to tell you.'

He stood up. 'Let's go down there,' he said, pointing to the sliding doors at the end of the carriage.

The four of us walked along the aisle, through the doors and stood in the space between the carriages.

'OK. What is it? I can tell by your face something's wrong.'

Brad told him he had seen Dracula's men on the train. 'They must have got on at Glasgow. They're looking for us, I'm sure.'

Dad put his hand to his chin. 'How did they know we were here?'

'They could have been in that helicopter. Remember? They might have spotted us on the road to Lochailort.'

'But why would they be looking for a horse and cart?'

'I think there's a simpler explanation,' said Dad. 'The landlord of the pub was angry with Rab MacGillicuddy, remember. He could have telephoned Balfour – just to make trouble for Rab.'

'Or the Men in Black might have been out and about looking for us,' I said. 'After all, they'd seen us near Grandad's bothy.'

'True,' said Richard. 'They could have called at the pub to ask the landlord if he's seen anyone passing.'

'But why didn't they stop us before we boarded the train at Lochailort?'

It was only then that I remembered what I had seen. 'There were two men quarrelling with Mr MacGillicuddy outside the station. I bet they were asking him where we'd gone. By the time they'd finished arguing, the train must have left.'

'Right,' said Kirstie. 'It would be easy to find out that we had to change at Glasgow – so they drove at top speed in time to be there when we boarded the next train.'

'Or they could have used the helicopter.'

There were all sorts of possibilities. But the important thing now was to decide what we should do to avoid being spotted.

'The real problem is that the Sumo Wrestler

knows what we look like,' said Brad. 'We had an unfortunate meeting in the laboratory.'

'Then you'd both better put your heads down on the tables in front of your seats. Cover as much of your head as you can with your arms and pretend to be asleep.'

'How long for, Dad?'

'Till we get to Edinburgh.'

Oh no! An hour of pretending to be asleep. I was about to be bored rigid again. Still, Dad's idea was a good one – so what could I say?

'When we get to Edinburgh, I want us all to split up. Pretend we don't know each other. They can't follow seven people going different ways. We'll head for the castle, as planned. We all know what to tell them when we get there – so, if only some of us get through tonight, we'll have achieved our goal.' He reached into his pocket for a pen. 'Brad, I'll write a note for your parents. Pass it to them on your way back to your seat, will you?'

That done, Brad turned and walked away, clutching the note, and disappeared through the sliding doors. Dad gave Kirstie and me a hug and told us to take care and that he was proud of us. Then we went back to our seats.

Settling down for the last part of the journey, I crossed my fingers and hoped that nothing would stop me from delivering the disc.

I did exactly as Dad had said and put my head on the table burying it in my arms. Because my face was hidden, I didn't need to shut my eyes. This meant that I could look through the crack between my jumper and the table and see the floor of the aisle between the seats. This may not sound much, but it was better than nothing. I was able to watch the different shoes that went past – big ones, small ones, flat ones, high ones. When, halfway through the journey, a pair of big black shiny lace-ups walked by, I didn't feel so good. I was pretty sure they belonged to the Sumo Wrestler – and that made me shiver. I was tempted to close my eyes, but I didn't. I had to know if he was coming back. He was. Those boots went past again... then, ten minutes later, they came back for the third time... but this time they didn't go past – they stopped right next to me and I held my breath. I could feel his eyes on me, boring into the back of my neck. I could sense him wondering if I was the girl he'd seen on the island. The one that broke into the lab. The one that knocked him over, tied him up and left him. I broke into a sweat just thinking about it and when I felt a hand on my shoulder, I almost fainted away.

BING-BONG.

The public address system cut in.

A woman's voice announced, 'The train will shortly be arriving in Waverley Station, Edinburgh. Please remember to take all your belongings with you.'

I saw the shiny black boots move away and I breathed again.

When the train lurched to a stop, I raised my head slowly and looked around. Everyone was standing up, pulling on jackets and taking bags from the overhead shelves. The carriage was heaving with people who towered above me and I felt all the safer for it. The Sumo Wrestler was nowhere to be seen. I was ready to run.

Lizzie peered out from under the seat and I lifted her up so that I could carry her from the train.

'Go on, lassie,' said an old man. 'You take your dog through.' And he made a space so that I could go in front of him – which I thought was very kind. Other people helped, too, and I was off the train in no time.

Once I was out, I put Lizzie down and together we raced along the platform and up the slope onto Waverley Bridge, brightly lit and busy with holiday-makers. I pushed my way through the crowds, not looking back. If I was being followed, I didn't want to know.

I ran like the wind over the bridge and crossed the road into Cockburn Street, still running as fast as my legs would carry me towards Advocates Close. I knew it well. It was a passageway with a set of steep stone steps – fifty or sixty – leading up to the Royal Mile and the Castle. On one side of the steps were old buildings like ancient skyscrapers – back doors of houses, entrances of offices – very tall and spooky and blackened with age. On the other side were small, neglected gardens.

I stepped into the dark entrance of the Close and leant against the wall, recovering my breath, preparing to climb the steps. The disc pressed against my chest and it felt good. Within the next few minutes, I would be handing it over to the authorities.

Chapter Twenty-Nine

What I didn't know was that Sumo had already seen me on the platform at the station. I had been in front of the crowd: a girl with a dog, running for her life. Easy to spot. He must have followed me.

In the shadow of Advocates Close, I felt confident that I had got away. But, before I started to climb the steps, something made me look back onto the street. That was when I saw him crossing the road and heading towards the Close. He was only a few metres behind me.

I was faster than he was, that was certain. I took a deep breath and started to run. with Lizzie at my heels. The first few steps were undercover and in darkness but, after that, the Close swung at right angles towards the Royal Mile. That part was open to the sky and lit with lamps.

The old stone steps were steep. Up...up...up... Before long, my legs had turned to jelly and there was a pounding inside my head I couldn't ignore. I couldn't run any longer.

Sumo had turned into the Close by then and I could hear his boots on the lower steps. Once he'd turned the corner into the light, he would see me, for sure.

To one side were tiny gardens, enclosed by low iron railings. They were horribly neglected, overgrown or filled with rubbish – just the place for me to hide. I clambered over into one garden and I flung myself low, dragging Lizzie with me so that we were hidden by the weeds and seeding grasses. Unfortunately, I landed in a clump of nettles and I had to bite my hand to stop me yelling as the stings began to burn into my skin. Somehow I managed to keep still and hold my breath for fear that Sumo might hear me panting. I wrapped my arms round Lizzie and held her close, making sure she didn't bark. The footsteps were nearer now. I trembled with the effort of keeping hidden – but when I heard him hurry by at last, I relaxed and felt a fantastic sense of relief sweep over me as I gulped air into my lungs.

Of course, there was always the chance that when Sumo realised that he had lost me, he might guess what I had done. I wondered if I should go back down the steps and take another route – but no, not yet. I would wait in the weed-filled garden for a bit longer.

I was still crouched there when it started to rain. Not heavy rain – just the usual Scottish drizzle. I waited, getting cold and wet. The drizzle clung to my clothes and the grass and the weeds. I wanted to stand up, shake off the wet. But I didn't. I waited.

Sumo didn't come back. By now he would be on the Royal Mile and that went right up to the castle – the way I needed to go – but at least there would be plenty of tourists and it would be difficult for him to spot me on the crowded pavements. There was safety in numbers. I hoped.

I took my time climbing the rest of the steps which were slippery with rain. The old streetlamps gave an eerie light to the Close, made more so by the reflections on the rain-soaked stone, black and shiny like a seal's back. I was near to the top when Lizzie suddenly stopped in her tracks and growled. To my left was a large door set back so it was in deep shadow. Even so, I strained my eyes to see what had caught Lizzie's attention. It was a large pile of rubbish, dirty clothes thrown out and left to rot. They were an eyesore. I was about to walk on when I saw the pile of rubbish move. My feet were glued to the spot as I stared and trembled, wondering if my imagination had taken hold of me. The bundle moved again. This time Lizzie barked, pulling at her lead so that I almost fell over. Then a man, bearded and fearsome, emerged from the heap. A bottle went flying out from the doorway, narrowly missing Lizzie and smashing at my feet.

'Take yer poxy dog away!' the man shouted in a thick gravel voice and he flung a tin at us. Lizzie lunged forward again, barking. 'Can't a man get some sleep around here?'

I tugged on the lead and dragged Lizzie away and ran to get out of his throwing range. He was nothing to do with me and I was nothing to do with him. All I wanted was to get out of the Close. It was a weird and scary place.

At the top of the steps a tunnel led onto the Royal Mile and I could already hear the sound of people walking along, talking and laughing – enjoying a night out in Edinburgh. I desperately wanted to rush out and run towards the castle. But I knew that this would be stupid. I needed to stop and peep round the corner to see whether Sumo or Trudor were near. It would have been a crazy thing to bump into them.

The dim lamps in the Close didn't reach into the tunnel and it was as black as pitch as I walked towards the opening.

'Ally!'

That was Kirstie's voice.

'Ally! I'm over here.'

Lizzie was yelping with excitement and when my eyes adjusted to the darkness, I saw my sister, her back pressed against the wall.

'What are you doing there?'

'Shhh! Keep your voice down. Lizzie, quiet!'

'OK, but nobody's listening.' I told her what had happened. 'Sumo followed me from the station but he went past me when I hid in a garden. He must be out there somewhere.'

'I know.'

'You mean you've seen him?'

'He's with another man. He's got red hair.'

'That's Brush Head. The boss man at the lab.'

'Yeah, well, he was using his mobile. There could be more of them. He was probably making contact with the others. I ducked in here to keep out of their way.'

'Sumo almost caught me.'

'You'd better give me the disc. I'm less likely to get caught.'

'Don't even ask, Kirstie. I'm going to get through.'

'Then I'll take Lizzie. You're too easily spotted with a dog.'

Reluctantly I agreed to give her up. I could see it was the right thing to do. A girl with a black and white dog in a crowd of tourists would stand out like an icicle in a desert.

'You need to change your appearance, Ally. You'd better have my sweater.'

I protested. Kirstie's sweater was pink with love hearts across the front. How girlie is that? It was too big anyway – halfway to my knees – but she insisted I put it on.

'You'll be freezing in your T-shirt,' I said. 'My sweater won't fit you.'

'I'll manage.'

The plan was for me to go out into the Royal Mile by myself, walking with groups of tourists if I could and heading for the castle. Kirstie would follow some way behind, keeping a lookout for Sumo, Trudor and any men who were with them. She was prepared to create a diversion if necessary.

'OK, Kirst. See you at the castle, I hope. Be good, Lizzie.'

After making sure there were no familiar faces in the street, I stepped out of Advocates Close and joined a group of French students who were standing on the pavement talking loudly and waving their arms and pointing. One would point up the road. The next would flap a hand to dismiss that idea and the next would point in the opposite direction. They were getting soaked, too. I stood behind them, waiting until they made up their mind where they should go. If they went uphill, I would stay with them. It would be a brilliant disguise. Who would look for me among a group of foreign students?

When they finally moved off, they headed in the direction of the castle as I had hoped. So far, so good. They walked quickly and I had to run to keep up but I felt safe and, best of all, I could see the castle floodlights lighting up the night sky. The castle itself was not far away now. It was the end of my journey.

What I didn't expect was that the students would cross over and walk into the Deacon Brodie's Tavern. All I could do was follow like a sheep, hoping they'd just have a swift drink and carry on up the hill. My brain was obviously not in gear that night. They most likely planned to be there until closing time.

Inside, the barman soon spotted me. 'Hey, wee lassie! You're too young to be here. You'll get me shot. Where's your mammy?'

Everyone turned to look at me, including the students, who had no idea I'd been trailing them. I wanted someone to say, 'She's with me' or 'Oh, it's only our Ally.' But, of course, no one did. I was alone and felt like a real idiot in the middle of the pub. I ran for the door and out into the street, where I found myself standing on an empty pavement. The tourists had thinned out with the rain and I was exposed for anyone to see. A ten-year-old girl alone at that time of night. If Sumo was within a hundred metres he was sure to spot me. There was nowhere to hide.

Chapter Thirty

What was I waiting for? I could be at the castle in no time. All I had to do was run.

The pub was on the corner of the Royal Mile and Bank Street where the traffic rushed towards George IV Bridge. Before I could go anywhere, I had to wait for the lights to change and the traffic to stop. I glanced behind me to see if I was being followed. Fifty metres or so down the Royal Mile I spotted Sumo. I groaned at the sight of him. He was pushing his way through a group of people, and behind him was Brush Head.

I felt desperate. The lights were still green. Still green. It felt like forever. I had come this far but would my luck hold out any longer?

Finally the lights turned red, the cars screeched to a halt on the wet road and I DASHED across. As I did so, I slipped on the wet tarmac. SPLAT! I was suddenly spread-eagled on the ground. Worse still, the disc had fallen out of its hiding place under my T-shirt and landed some way away. I scrambled to my feet before the lights changed and the traffic started to move again, panicking that Sumo might be catching up with me. I reached the disk and picked it up before racing on towards the castle.

I was just minutes away from the Esplanade, a huge flat space spread in front of the castle. I ran and ran, pumping my arms. They weren't going to catch me now – not Sumo . . . not Brush Head . . . not the rest of them.

Up to the Esplanade. I kept going. All I had to do was cross it and I'd be there at the gates of Edinburgh Castle. I raced across the flat space, my feet flying over the tarmac. The blood was pounding in my head so loudly that I wasn't aware of the whirring sound above me. Not until it came much closer. Then the noise of a helicopter filled the air and I looked up and saw it dropping from the sky like a sycamore seed. It was the helicopter we had seen on the way to Lochailort. It was landing on the Esplanade. I skidded to a halt, unable to believe what I saw, unable to move.

Alarms sounded from the castle as it landed. Searchlights on the battlements were directed onto the helicopter and soldiers on guard at the gate came rushing forward with guns at the ready. But when the doors of the chopper were flung open, Men in Black leapt out to face them, carrying huge automatic weapons and outnumbered them two to one.

The last person to emerge was none other than Dracula himself. It felt like the end for me. My feet were rooted to the spot. Dracula looked darker and more evil than ever. He made my skin creep.

'Alexandra,' he called across. 'I've been hoping to meet you. I think you have something that belongs to me.'

He held out his hand for the disc and for a moment I was paralysed with fear.

But I suddenly came to my senses. If he thought he was going to get it, he could go fly a kite. I spun round – ready for off. I raced away in the opposite direction – right slap bang into Sumo's stomach – winding him, but not enough to do any serious damage, unfortunately. He grabbed my arm and pulled it hard behind my back. I bet he really enjoyed that – paying me for the time we tied him up with that plastic bag. Then Brush Head turned up, breathless after running up the road, and together they dragged me over to the helicopter where Dracula was waiting.

'Get rid of those soldiers, Trudor,' Dracula said. 'Tell them to drop their weapons or I shall kill the girl.' Sumo had released me but Dracula was pointing a revolver at my head. I had never been this close to a gun and I didn't like it!

Brush Head did what he was told. Barking an order at the soldiers. But instead of dropping their guns, they only lowered them – which wasn't good news for me. I didn't think much of my chances of escape. If the soldiers fired, I'd get a bullet from Dracula's gun. Curtains for me.

'Get the men back into the helicopter,' Dracula snapped. 'We've got what we wanted. We'll take the girl with us as a hostage.'

Once the Men in Black had climbed in, Dracula waved his gun in the direction of the open door.

'Get in!' he shouted.

The blades were whirring round and I could hardly stand for the force of the wind. It was like a hurricane. But I stayed put.

'GET IN!' he shouted again.

When I wouldn't move he grabbed my arm and dragged me, kicking and screaming, across the tarmac.

This was Dracula's biggest mistake!

Unknown to me, Kirstie had arrived and was standing not far away watching everything that was going on. So was Lizzie. When she saw I was in trouble, she went mad and broke away from Kirstie. She tore across the Esplanade like a hairy missile. She latched onto Dracula's leg, biting through to the bone so that he screamed. He dropped the gun. He dropped the disc. He tried to get free of Lizzie's teeth but there was no way she would loose her grip. I grabbed the disc, picked up the gun and pointed it at the scumbag doctor. This stopped any of his men attempting to climb out of the helicopter. They were dead scared that I'd fire.

After that, the world went mad. The soldiers from the castle ran towards us, weapons raised. More soldiers burst through the gates and surrounded the helicopter. Police cars drove up the Royal Mile, sirens blaring, and two military helicopters arrived deafening everybody as they circled overhead before landing. It looked as though Dr Frankwall and his men had been well and truly caught.

Chapter Thirty-One

Dad and Grandad came running across the Esplanade. So did Brad and his parents. Just as we planned, we had come our separate ways and we'd all made it to the castle.

Dad put his arms round me and hugged me to bits.

'I'm OK, Dad,' I said. Of course I was.

But that wasn't the end of it. Suddenly we found ourselves surrounded by a group of soldiers pointing guns at *us*. I went ballistic. What was all that about? We'd delivered a dangerous man, a threat to society, a terrorist – and *we* were being arrested! *We* were being treated like *we* were the enemy! How crazy was that?

Dad put his hand on my shoulder. 'Give them the gun, Ally. Don't be angry. They need to know who we are and why we're here. Remember, the Parliament Building was blown up by terrorists. They need to be watchful.'

A man in an officer's uniform marched over. 'Take them in. Quick as you can.'

'To the castle. Quick march,' snapped one of the soldiers and pointed his gun at the gate.

'We'll have to go with them, Ally,' Dad said. 'It'll be OK. Come on.'

I was crazy with rage. We were marched like criminals past the helicopters, down the Esplanade and through the massive stone gateway. Once we were through, the gates were slammed shut, cutting us off from the outside world. We were taken across the courtyard to a door in the stone wall that led to a sort of police station – except it was staffed by soldiers. Then – and this was the worst thing of all – we were put in cells. We were separated – I guess so we couldn't talk to each other. They do that with criminals. I've seen it on TV. Only Kirstie and I were put together – probably because we were young and they didn't think kids were important.

Nothing happened for ages and ages until a soldier came into our cell and took us down a long corridor to see a man called Colonel Brodie who was in charge. He was in a square room with no windows and walls that were bare except for a camera fixed high up and pointing to the table and chairs in the middle. Colonel Brodie was sitting on the far side of the table. He was tall, with a large nose and small dark eyes.

'Please take a seat,' he said, pointing to the chairs opposite.

Then Dad came in. He looked fine. Why was he in such a good mood? It's not every day that you get arrested, accused of being a terrorist and put into a cell.

'The Colonel has asked me to sit with you both while you tell him what you know. I've told him what I know and Brad and his parents have done the same. Just tell him what you saw on the island.'

The Colonel leaned across the table and smiled at me, revealing a large gap between his front two teeth. 'Your father tells me you have something that is very, very important,' he said as if he was speaking to a five-year-old. 'Perhaps you could put it on the table like a good girl.'

When I copied the data onto the disc, I swore that I would only give it to someone in the government. Someone powerful. Otherwise, why would we have come all this way to the castle? The information was of massive importance and now this officer wanted me to pass it over like a bag of sweets to be looked over and shared around. I don't think so.

I sat back in my chair and folded my arms. 'No,' I said. 'I need to see the First Minister.'

Dad look amazed. So did the Colonel. Kirstie looked impressed and her mouth twitched into a hint of a smile. After that there was a lot of talking and blustering, saying that what I'd asked for was impossible.

'All you've got to do is make a phone call,' I said. 'Tell him what's going on.'

The Colonel was not a happy bunny. His ears had turned pink and he was beginning to sweat. 'The First Minister knows exactly what's going on, young lady. He saw what happened in the Esplanade. He has already interviewed Dr Frankwall and he is waiting in his office for me to give him the information you have brought.'

'Why can't I give it to him myself?'

'Yes, why can't she?' Kirstie asked.

'You are rather too...er...young. It will be better coming from me.'

I was furious and slammed my fists on the desk, which made him jump. 'I wasn't too young to get the information from the doctor's computer. So I'm not too young to give it to the First Minister. If I can't give it to him, you're not having it.'

The Colonel was gritting his teeth and his face had turned an unnatural shade of red. 'Look here.

You can't dictate to me like that. I won't have it.'

'Then I'll go.' I stood up and ran for the door. The soldier standing next to it was taken by surprise and didn't move fast enough to stop me getting out. Kirstie knew what to do. She told me afterwards that she shut the door, flung a chair across it and sat on it. Then she started to scream. Soldiers came running to the interview room to see what was going on which meant that they didn't chase me and I had a few extra seconds in which to find the way to the First Minister's office.

Edinburgh Castle has been a fortress for hundreds of years so it made a safe place in which to house the government. In fact, when they had such a brilliant place to begin with, why did they bother to build the new Parliament Building?

I easily found the part of the castle with the offices of the Members of the Scottish Parliament and the First Minister himself. Bad luck that there was a guard on the door. But this was where my acting skills came in handy. I pretended I was just an innocent girl wandering around the castle when she ought to be in bed. It was the best I could do at the time.

'Hello,' I said. 'I'm here with my dad.'

'Oh yeah? Who's your dad then?'

'A very important man.'

'Really?'

'Yes, he reads lots and lots of reports and signs lots and lots of papers.'

'Very interesting, I'm sure.'

'I've brought something for the First Minister.'

'You can't see him. Now hop it. Go back to your dad.'

Just then, the alarm system sounded round the castle. The whole place seemed to erupt – probably looking for me. Two soldiers came haring across the quadrangle shouting to the guard but he couldn't make out what they were saying for the noise that the alarm system was making.

'What's going on?' he called and walked forward to meet them.

This was just the chance I needed. I stepped behind him and slipped in through the door, slamming it shut and throwing the bolt across it. In front of me was a long corridor with doors on either side and I ran down looking from side to side until I saw the door with a large label that read: FIRST MINISTER. Without pausing to knock, I pushed the door open and found myself in a huge room. There, sitting at a desk reading a pile of papers, was the First Minister himself. He looked up, put his pen on his desk and leaned forward.

'Ah,' he said. 'You are Alexandra Dunbar, are you not?'

I nodded. There was nothing else to do but walk up to the desk and put the disc right in front of him.

He smiled and picked it up. 'And I believe I know what this is. Thank you.'

I stood there like an idiot not knowing what to say.

'But,' he continued, 'I shall have to send for my scientific advisers before we look at it. They will understand it more than I.' He picked up the phone and made a call.

The advisers were with us in a flash. None of them said, 'Sorry, I'm busy writing a report' or 'Can it wait till tomorrow?' or 'I'm watching a match on telly'. No. Nothing like that. When the most powerful man in Scotland called, they came running.

There were three of them, all wearing glasses, and they stood behind the First Minister, leaning forward so they could see the computer on his desk. One put the disc into the slot and waited to see the data I had copied.

As they scrolled through it, their lips tightened and their faces grew grim.

'I cannot believe what I'm reading,' the first scientist said. 'This man has learned to control the weather. Impossible!'

'See here,' another said, pointing at the screen. 'He has actually done experiments to raise the temperature of the sea.'

'He can create hurricanes. It's incredible!'

The First Minister stood up. 'Alexandra, do you realise that Dr Frankwall is a terrorist of the greatest magnitude? He could ruin cities – whole countries, if he wanted to. You, my young woman, have saved us all from this evil man. You and your friends shall have our undying thanks.'

Chapter Thirty-Two

Before Brad and his family went home to California, we all went back to the island with some people from the military and the police.

When we landed, we saw at once that Caitlin was a ghost village. All the houses were gone and the one thing left standing was the old red telephone box. Later, the council decided that it should stay there in memory of those who died.

Away from the village, they found the Camerons' farm and Grandad's cottage flattened as we had told them. But a soldier climbed down into the cellar and brought out most of my fossil collection. Cool!

When we went over to the far side of the island, we found Brad's boat still anchored near the cave – but there was no sign of the vultures. Best of all, we discovered Dobbin, happily grazing on the hillside. He went galloping round in circles – he was really glad to see us. Good old Dobbin. We took him to the mainland on the ferry and Rab MacGillicuddy offered to keep him on his farm where he would have other horses for company. So that was all right.

For weeks after that, there were loads of

questions they wanted us to answer and then, once the enquiries were over, Brad and his parents decided to go back to the States. They had made sense of what Brad's uncle had first discovered. They had ended the investigation he had begun.

'This has sure been an exciting holiday,' Brad said. 'I'm gonna miss you guys.'

'Can we come and see you?' I asked.

Kim laughed. 'Of course. Come whenever you like.'

'And Grandad? Can he come?'

But Grandad shook his head. 'I dunno,' he said. 'It's a long way from Scotland.'

'Think of it as an adventure,' said Dad.

'Ach, I've had enough adventures to last me a lifetime.'

'Then come to California for the sunshine and the fishing,' said Kim.

Grandad's face lit up with a wide, beaming smile. 'Aye. Now you're talking, lassie.'

Richard laughed. 'Then we'll be delighted to see you all.'

So we agreed to go the following summer. After all our troubles, that was something good to look forward to, don't you think?